Praise for J. Mercer's women's fiction:

After They Go

"...Mercer's prose is lucid and her themes of redemption and reinvention are resonant..."

— *Kirkus Reviews*

"Mercer's story is set in a struggling tumbleweed of a beach town, with one family at its center. Passing time is marked by emotionally traumatic or uplifting events, which are exceptionally well conveyed through Mercer's delicate plotting. Mercer's prose flows through this beach town family saga quite smoothly and evocatively. Meticulous descriptions capture circumstances both mundane and exceptional–death, loss of innocence, proclamations of love, starting over, and rebuilding broken lives. Characters are intricately woven, unique, and relatable."

— *The BookLife Prize*

"Mercer's prose is solid, evoking a strong sense of character and place that adds intensity and texture to the narrative... Gwen's and Betta's storylines will appeal to fans of women's fiction, while Ez's narrative will satisfy those looking for a coming-of-age story. Overall, readers who enjoy family sagas will find After They Go an engaging read."

— *OnlineBookClub.org*

Also by J. Mercer:

After They Go

Dark & Stormy

Triplicity

J. Mercer

Published 2019 / Bare Ink
Printed in the United States of America
Print ISBN: 978-1-7321332-4-2
E-ISBN: 978-1-7321332-5-9
Library of Congress Control Number: 2107469
Triplicity / written by J. Mercer

Cover design © Robin Vuchnich
Edited by Rochelle Melander

For Joel, my fun and enthusiasm;
I heart the Jesse in you.

ITINERARY

Day 1: Boarding
Boat departs at 4:00 p.m.

Day 2: At sea

Day 3: Ketchikan
6:30 a.m. – 3:00 p.m.

Day 4:
Tracy Arm Fjord (scenic cruising)
5:00 a.m. – 9:00 a.m.
Juneau
12:30 p.m. – 10:00 p.m.

Day 5: Skagway
6:00 a.m. – 5:00 p.m.

Day 6: At sea

Day 7: At sea
Victoria, British Columbia
7:00 p.m. – 11:59 p.m.

Day 8:
Arrive in Seattle at 7:00 a.m.
Disembark by 11:00a.m.

triplicity:
[trih-*plis*-i-tee]
noun, plural: triplicities
1. the quality or state of being triple; threefold character or condition.
2. a group or combination of three; triad.
3. "There are three sides to every story—your side, my side, and the truth."
—Robert Evans

Day 1: Boarding

Boat departs at 4:00 p.m.

Navy

Masses of people stood in line to board the incubator in front of me. Sorry, cruise ship. But honestly, the thought of so many bodily fluids in such a confined space made my stomach churn.

Double-checking that my hand sanitizer was still in place, I bumped my backpack higher on my shoulder and stepped away from my mom's fiancé, who was chatting up a blue-haired old lady. Facing my mom, I decided it was as good a time as any to start up our fight again. She couldn't get away from me here.

"If we keep moving like this," I started, "I'll never be kissed." There'd been one guy in Houston I'd had hopes for, but after this vacation we were headed to Kansas City. I might only be sixteen and five-sixths, but at this point it felt like I'd be voting first.

"You do the kissing then, Navy." My mom caught the eye of an officer at the next checkpoint and smiled, smoothing her hands down the front of her black jumpsuit. She was always worried about her first impression and always deferential to those in uniform.

I reached behind her and tightened her halter top, thankful at least she hadn't picked the leopard print. It was a good thing we were getting out of Texas before its fashion sense could get too many claws in her.

My mom's normal go-to attire—conservative diamond studs, fitted sweaters with pencil skirts, and sleek suits— would curl a lip at sharing suitcase space with a glorified onesie in leopard print.

Her attention hopped from the officer to Guy, my soon-to-be stepdad. "Solve your own problems, dear. Before they can solve you."

"No, Mom. Just, no." She would never get it; everyone wanted to kiss her. Somehow, she pulled off rich and cultured while still approachable, where my resting face was icy at best.

A girl couldn't help her resting face, and it took a long time for people to get past that. Plus, I was too picky, or so my mother said. I wanted real emotion, not just chemistry, and I definitely didn't want to get it over with, which is what she kept telling me to do.

"Anyway, this move,"—always moving, I should add—"it's

about stability too."

Guy let out a huge laugh, and the old lady's hat bobbled in the air as her shoulders shook. My mom and I shuffled forward, neither of us bothering to notify him he was holding up the line. It didn't matter; this was the Godzilla of lines. Take any ride at Disney on the busiest day of the year, and it wouldn't top this one: through a vast building (stand here, punch that, sign this, rude hands gesturing you impatiently over there like you'd done this before and had any idea what they wanted with you), out into a human holding tank, up and back and up and forth inside a humongous steel cage, until finally we reached the deck that wrapped around the massive boat.

We were cattle. And we were being herded into an incubator.

Shaking my head of it, I begged her, "Please, please, *please* don't make me switch high schools again. This is the last one, okay? Can you manage two years in Kansas City?"

"If you insist, love." My mom patted the back of my head, then dropped her hand to my shoulder and kneaded it. With her attention focused elsewhere, it was her usual absent-minded pep talk. "If you don't want to see more of the world."

Shaking her off, I took a few steps forward. Guy was still flirting with the old lady and people were starting to grumble behind them, so I went back for his stuff and tapped him on the shoulder. His black turtleneck made him look even more pompous than he was, but this lady was eating it up same as my mom had. When I was back at her side, I whispered, "If you get sick of Guy, we stay in Kansas City anyway. Got it?"

She extended her diamond-studded right hand to shake mine. "Got it."

Wrapping my bare fingers around her chilled palm and the collection of old rings resting along her knuckles, I wondered if she actually loved this one.

Isaiah

The ship was so big. As big as a mountain. But I was used to twenty people on a mountain, not a million people inside one.

I craned my neck to get a better look at the girl ten or so people ahead of us. Of course, Gram thought I was watching the pretty boy with the sparkling teeth and preppy outfit.

"Keep your eyes in your head, Zay," she muttered.

It didn't matter how many times I told her I liked girls. She couldn't imagine why else I'd want to work with an all-male ranch staff in the middle of nowhere, Montana.

The girl's blonde hair was a shiny mane, and her outfit—dark skinny jeans, a white tee, and huge turquoise earrings—was perfect: no frills, no bullshit.

Gram swatted me with her purse. I glared at her.

"Nice to have a week off, Zay?" My great-aunt Ethel asked.

We were here on her dime, bought company for an old woman, so I muttered out a response and went back to the hair. My fingers twitched to feel it. Not in a creepy way, but brushing out horses was the most relaxing part of my day.

"He's got more 'an a week," Gram said. "I'm not sendin' him back."

My throat dried up. She couldn't be serious.

"I mean it too." Nodding, she grabbed her suitcase. Marched forward a few paces.

I hurried after her. "I can't quit in the middle of a summer with no notice. Ike needs me."

"I gave Ike your notice the day you left. He knows."

"Why would you do that?"

Hands on her hips. "You had a girlfriend yet?"

"Yes!"

"Yeah, right. I know how many of them're up at that ranch."

"Gram, I'm watching that blonde girl, okay?" I pointed over her head. The boy who was way too preppy for me turned. He put up a few fingers and waved.

"That prissy one with the frown?" Ethel asked. "She looks mean."

"Oh, he's just tellin' me what he knows I wanna hear. Tellin' time's over, Zay. You need to get your life together."

"What's wrong with my life?" What I had was what I wanted. All I'd ever want. My fist clenched. I couldn't lose the ranch, not after I'd lost everything else.

"Them boys aren't gonna make you a family, and that ranch ain't gonna make you a future." She shuffled her feet forward.

I pulled my cowboy hat down. The blonde was slipping inside the ship anyway. "They *are* my family, and if being a grunt ranch hand is my future, I'm happy with that."

"I'm your family," she snapped. "And you're happy with it because you're seventeen and you don't know no better."

"Gram, please?" It was a desperate whisper.

"It's all the poor boy has left," Aunt Ethel pointed out, not looking at me. Not even for a second. As if I might miss that I was the poor boy she was talking about.

Gram crossed her arms. "Building his future is more important than what he does or does not have left."

"Other people we know have been gay," Aunt Ethel said. "Jeannie from the corner, for example, and you never worried about her future."

Gram glared at her. "Jeannie wasn't my grandson."

"Then make me a deal," I said, because this was something we did.

"Yes." Aunt Ethel smiled before turning back to Gram. "He gets a girlfriend, you let him go back."

Gram looked like she was face-to-face with a skunk. "What's a girlfriend gonna prove?"

"For one, it'll prove he likes girls."

"He can right fake that. Anyway, there's more 'an one reason I don't want him at that ranch."

"Give the boy some hope, Liza. He's only seventeen. He's still got time to work his life out."

Gram eyed me for a full two minutes. I counted the ticks in my head while studying the wooden decking, how it barely moved beneath my feet. Hope was suddenly the color of that girl's hair, and I talked myself into wanting the rest of her too, no matter what she ended up being. Because now, with Gram's curt nod, it seemed she was the only way I'd get back home.

Jesse

"I am not sleeping there," I said, throwing my suitcase on the one queen bed in the room and heading to the patio doors that led to a tiny deck. "Mom should be sleeping there, and I won't take her spot."

We were pulling away from port, and the skyline of Seattle stretched in front of me like a postcard or a puzzle. Futzing with the lock, I opened the door and stepped out to take a picture.

"Only for photos!" my dad called, a reminder not to use my phone. I could barely hear him, though, over the hum of the engine and the slapping of the waves against the boat. The downside to taking a ship to sea? No cell towers, roaming charges, and very expensive Wi-Fi.

I went back inside but left the door open for the fresh air. Well, arguably fresh. The odor of big city tainted the briny scent coming off the water, but soon enough we'd be able to fill our noses with it.

"Stupid to have them pull out that couch for you every night." Unzipping his luggage, my dad motioned me over and nudged my suitcase. "I won't spoon you, don't worry."

Sliding into the little hall by the bathroom, he returned with hangers. As he slid his dress clothes onto them, I could tell by the muscles hardening his brightly-colored biceps that he wasn't as cool with the whole situation as he looked. Why was I giving him a hard time anyway? She was leaving us both.

I swallowed. "Why'd she surprise us with a trip if she wasn't going to come?"

"So she wouldn't have to face us."

My crisp dress shirt crumpled in my fist.

"If we were there when she was moving out, we'd have made her feel more guilty." His words were radio static, strange and wrong and scraping. I regretted asking the question.

He motioned for the items I'd hung up, then went back to the closet. A few moments passed, longer than it took to hang a few shirts on a rod. I'd never seen my dad cry, but there'd been a few times on the drive here when I thought he might lose it. The thing was, though, her stuff had been in all the right places when I'd been packing, and she'd been there when we pulled out of the driveway. For all we knew, no matter what she said, she might still be there when we got back.

A knock shook the door, and with three strides, Dad had it open. A short, slight man stood in front of him, in yet another uniform. There'd been no shortage of people today and no shortage of uniforms.

"Hi sirs. I will like to introduce myself to you, your cabin attendant this week." He nodded, but I knew my dad couldn't hear him over the accent. Which made them even, as likely our cabin attendant couldn't hear my dad over his tattoos. Most people couldn't.

I stepped up to shake his hand and repeated him for my father's sake. "You're our cabin attendant this week?"

He pumped my arm and nodded with the same beat. "Anything you need. I help. Every night I pull down sheets. Turn down service, chocolates. I bring your bags to your door. I take them out for you at end of week. Have a question? You find me." He motioned up and down the hall, like that's where he'd be.

Checking his nametag, I said, "It's nice to meet you, Danilo."

"Da-NEE-lo," he corrected my pronunciation with a smile.

"I'm Jesse Kowalski." I thumbed toward my dad, who'd slipped back into the tiny hall. "That's my dad. People call him Wally."

Dad rolled his eyes and turned away. He hated when I chatted with people.

"Is only the two of you?" he asked, peering in as if he could see into our past two weeks.

Dad made a garbled noise, and I nodded.

"I will split bed, okay?" He motioned toward it.

"Oh. You can do that?"

"Yes, sir. Sorry to have made mistake."

"There was, um, no mistake," I assured.

"I'll split when you are at dinner, yes?"

"That's great, Danilo, thanks." Nodding, I hung a hand on top of the open door. "Hey, where you from?"

"Philippines, Jesse. You?"

"Omaha, Nebraska. Ever heard of it?"

"No, sir."

"Center of the U.S. Land-locked. Know what I mean?"

He shook his head, a wrinkle creasing between his brows.

"So far inland, no sea in sight." He seemed a little confused, so I moved on. "You leave anyone behind in the Philippines?"

"I don't think those are the kinds of questions he was talking about, Jess," my dad grumbled from the bed.

"I have wife. Five boys. One girl. Many sisters too."

"How long are you here then, working on the boat?" Dropping my arm, I leaned against the door. "When do you go home?"

"Six months. Then home six months."

"Yeah? The pay good?"

"Oh, yes. Lots of money for easy living in the Philippines."

I nodded. That's what I'd do. I'd pretend my mom was working on a cruise ship. Six months on and six months off sounded like a way better reason for her not to be here. Maybe then it wouldn't hurt so bad, the tears my dad hadn't shed that were scraping me raw anyway.

Navy

"Don't be a party pooper, Navy. The teen lounge has all sorts of fun activities planned for your enjoyment."

"That's exactly the problem, Mom. The people who say they've planned fun activities for my enjoyment don't know what fun is."

We were waiting in line (ugh, the lines!) to enter the dining room, where apparently we'd eat every meal at the same table with the same people, probably a bunch of old ladies, and I'd have to listen to Guy chatting them up seven nights in a row.

At least he'd known how to find the dining hall. As he kept saying, this wasn't his first rodeo. Mom and I had been walking in circles before he'd caught up to us. Granted, we'd been distracted with the fancy staircases and glitzy central piazza, but the Venetian Ballroom was also situated in a rather shadowy alcove.

And Venetian it was, if I took the paintings hung along the paneled wooden walls to be accurate: boats and water, squat buildings and looming mountains, a woman in a poufy blouse and full skirt bent in an awkward position over a copper bucket.

I followed my mom, who followed Guy, who followed a host to our table. The host pulled out a chair for my mom, and the waiter, already in position, pulled one out for me.

"Thank you." I nodded. He was tall and broad with intense, beady eyes.

"You're welcome, Miss." Oh, but he had a lovely accent.

The many different native tongues were an unexpected bonus of this cruise. Like Vegas, where each nametag listed a home state, the nametags on this ship listed a home country. How many languages could I keep track of at one time? And how much could I soak up in a week?

"Guy!" an old lady shrieked from behind me, before I could awkwardly ask our host how they'd say 'You're welcome' in Hungarian. "What a surprise!"

"Ethel! So lovely to see you again!" Guy stood up and took both of her red-tipped hands in his. "We couldn't have planned it better!"

He pulled out her chair, and I looked up to find she wasn't as old as her voice made her sound, maybe sixties. Ten years older than Guy and twenty more than my mom. She was a hippy kind of trendy with long, curly gray hair. There was a cute old lady with her, and a teenager. A male teenager, in fact, with lips. That covered two of the three necessary kissing ingredients, the third being some sort of emotional connection. Could I find that in a week?

He tipped his cowboy hat at me. It was a nice one too, if I'd learned anything in the five months we'd been in Texas.

"Who's with you, Guy? I think we saw this lovely girl in

line." Ethel squinted at me. "Zay, didn't we see her in line?"

The cowboy with the wholesome farm boy face reached his hand over the table. "Isaiah. They call me Zay."

I didn't take it. Who knew if he had ever-a-virus, or whatever it was going around. "Navy Carmichael," I replied instead, forcing out a smile so I wouldn't seem completely rude.

Isaiah's hand hung there while Guy and Ethel finished introductions. The old lady was Isaiah's grandmother Liza, and Ethel was her sister. Then there were the vomit-worthy congrats-I-didn't-even-know-you-were-engaged coos.

"How do you know each other?" I asked Guy and Ethel. "I mean, how *would* you have known he was engaged?"

Ethel and Liza stared at me, and my mom patted my thigh. "Baby, it's just something people say to be nice."

"We met on my first cruise, many years ago." Ethel smiled at Guy. "He showed me the ropes, and we've been bumping into each other ever since. That was Turkey and Greece, right?"

Dang, how come we had to be going to Alaska?

"It was. You won the jackpot that trip." He elbowed her. "Ethel's a Bingo shark, ladies. Watch out for her."

My mom leaned closer to Guy but set her interested face on Ethel. "You'll have to show me some tricks. I've heard Bingo is exhilarating."

"You've never played?" Liza asked.

"Don't worry," Mom assured her. "I plan to start this week. I hear that's where the action is on these cruise ships."

Ethel and Liza studied her with blank faces. I agreed. She didn't seem much for action, with the perfectly smoothed hair and pearly fingernails. A slim white jacket was buttoned over her black jumpsuit, and a dainty gold necklace hung from her neck. The whole vibe screamed proper, high-class lady.

You could hardly see the pastor's wife anymore, or the Southern belle straight off a good old-fashioned plantation. Honestly, I missed them both.

Jesse

There were two chairs left at our assigned dinner table, and they sat between a cowboy and the most intimidating girl I'd ever seen. *Hi, I'm Navy*, she'd said, *Navy Carmichael*. She had a spattering of yellow-gold freckles on her face, the same color as her hair, which was rich and shiny like liquid gold, and they accented a severe expression I couldn't shake.

She had perfect posture, refused my handshake, and looked like she belonged with the fancy white tablecloths, fresh flower centerpieces, and glass goblets for water, of all things. Fifteen pieces of silverware per plate, each of us with a coffee cup, and a basket of rolls in the center of the table covered with more white cloth.

Back home, my mom threw a stack of buttered bread on a plate and called it a day.

As everyone introduced themselves, I tugged my t-shirt sleeve down over my tattooed bicep and slid my palm over the mustache on the back of my elbow. Rites of passage, seeing as the family business was an ink shop.

Navy caught me, and I played it off by strumming my fingers a bit. I couldn't read her expression, but no doubt she was labeling me from head to toe.

"What would you like to dine on this evening, sir?" The waiter asked.

He was a huge mountain of a man, but that'd never stopped me from opening my mouth before. And I'd never be able to look away from his nametag if I didn't ask. Reaching a hand out, I said, "I'm Jesse. Nice to meet you . . . ?"

"Balasz."

Ending with a soft J and emphasis on the second syllable, which he drew out, it sounded like Ba-*lahhj*. "What nationality?" I asked, trying to see around his arm at the rest of his nametag.

"Hungarian." He pressed tight a thin smile. "For you for dinner?"

"Oh, um." I glanced back at the menu. "I'll have the soup for starters. How're the scallops compared to the prime rib?"

He scribbled. "Soup, scallops, prime rib."

"Oh, no, not both. Which would you recommend?"

"Both." He took a step toward my dad.

"Balasz, I can't eat all that."

"No problem, Jesse. You eat what you can. Enjoy. Feast."

"No soup then, okay?"

"Oh, but soup is good. You'll see."

"Balasz."

He put his hand up. "Trust me."

Slumping back in my seat, I turned to Navy, who was smirking—but *with* me, I was pretty sure this time, not at me. I sighed into it, needing some sort of distraction.

I'd been leaving messages for my mom the whole drive out to Seattle, and ten minutes ago she finally texted me back.

A text.

I'll leave some soup in the fridge for when you get home, okay? This was a far cry from answering any of the questions I'd left on her voicemail.

My head shot back to my dad. "You did not just order a bourbon for dinner," I hissed, as Balasz moved on to Isaiah.

"Nope. I ordered three."

Isaiah

I'd thought about sitting next to her. But then I'd have been the creepy new guy. What were the odds there'd be another person our age at the table? He was twitchy at least. No way she'd go for that, classy show mare that she was. She might be trying to hide it with the white tee and jeans, but the way she held herself? There was no doubt.

Plus, he downed his entire meal like he was eating out of a trough.

Jesse pushed back in his seat. "I'm gonna head up to the teen lounge. You guys wanna come?"

I snorted, and Navy stared at him. Yeah, and he still felt the need to be babysat. I had this in the bag.

"All right, well, maybe I'll catch you later." Jesse glanced at his dad. Dude was staring into his third drink. "See you back at the room?"

Navy's mom—*It's Delilah, but you can call me Dee*—said, "Navy will go with you, dear. She was saying on the way in how enjoyable it sounded."

Navy rolled her head dramatically to stare at her mother. Delilah patted Navy's hand with a smile, then leaned in to whisper in her ear. Navy stood, tossing her napkin on the table.

I got up too. "If this is as lame as I think it's gonna be, we're out of there in fifteen minutes."

"Zay—"

"Yeah, Gram, I know." I cut her off before she could announce that I had a curfew. She wanted me back before she fell asleep. Said she spent enough time worrying about me when I was gone at the ranch.

Worry, worry, worry. She thought she could worry me happy. It made sense five years ago, but things were better now.

Nodding, she slipped her hand in mine and squeezed,

holding tight until I did the same. Which I did, to reassure her for all the times she'd used that squeeze to reassure me.

As soon as we were away from the table, Jesse started nickering. "Isn't this cool? I didn't actually think it would look like the Titanic, but it's like we're stuck in the movie. This is the crazy biggest ship I've ever been on, let alone seen. You guys ever been on a cruise before? I keep getting lost. It's like you need a compass in here . . ."

He was right. We didn't know how to get around. Took us ten times longer than it should have to find the elevator. Or felt like it because of his constant stream of consciousness.

When we finally swung into the right alcove, preppy boy from the line was there. Done up in an outfit that wouldn't last through a day of real work. He spotted Jesse first, since he was making all the noise. When he saw me, a smile busted out of his lips.

"Hey, Cowboy." He ran a hand through his hair. "You guys heading up to the teen lounge?"

"That we are," Jesse replied, reaching a hand out.

"Bern. Nice to meet you."

"Jesse." Nodding to drive this home, he motioned to Navy. "This is Navy, and the cowboy is Isaiah."

Bern rocked back on his dress shoes. "Isaiah's nice, but I prefer Cowboy."

Great. Just what I needed. And no way could I be a dick about it. I didn't have it in me.

I sidled closer to Navy, a hint for him if he were willing to notice it. She took a step away, like she could've sensed I was behind her even if she had blinders on. Maybe Aunt Ethel's first impression was right. Maybe she was mean and prissy.

"Do you know where we're going, Bern?" Navy asked, as the door dinged open.

"I sure do." He stepped onto the elevator. "Deck seventeen." Then he side-eyed Jesse's tattooed bicep. "You play piano or something?"

"No. I mean, someday hopefully. I'm just really into music. Instrumental, actually. And this was cooler than a violin. Violins might be my favorite. I love when it's just one instrument too, there's this lonely quality about it, you know? Like it's reaching out to speak to you—"

"You're an odd dude," Bern interrupted. "I think we're gonna get along just fine."

But he was looking at me when he said it.

Jesse

I ran my hand along the foosball table as we took in the open space: dark walls, huge windows, and a circle of couches set up around a double-sided entertainment center. A few kids were playing video games on one side, so I grabbed the controllers from the other.

"Anyone up for a game?" I asked.

"I'll watch," Navy said, kicking her sandals off and settling on the couch. Bending her knees, she pulled her feet up under her like she could be comfortable here as well as at a fancy dinner. It made her more real, a normal girl.

Bern grabbed a controller from my hand and went to start a game, while Isaiah sat next to Navy. The sound of my favorite game loaded behind me as Bern set his tan suit jacket on the couch and rolled up the arms of his button down shirt.

I laughed, because he didn't know what was coming; I was going to positively kill this.

"Get ready to shake those hips, Messy Jesse."

Messy? I smoothed my unruly curls and checked my shorts for wrinkles. Not that many, really. Did I have stains on my t-shirt? Nope. Granted, Bern was high gloss, but still. Frowning, I glanced at Navy, then spun toward the TV before I missed my turn.

One minute of slick dance moves later, Navy was clapping, a huge smile opening up her face, and Isaiah tipped his hat at me.

Bern whistled and hip-bumped me so he could take the stage. "I was not expecting such tough competition. Not at all."

"This girl at work used to make me dance all the time," I admitted. And my mom, she used to make me dance too.

"At work?" Navy asked.

"I'm a late night radio DJ." In one of the messages I'd left my mom, I asked her where she was moving. Like, did it have two bedrooms? Would she use the second bedroom as an office? An art room? A guest room for her sister?

I'll leave soup in the fridge for when you get home, okay?

"Wait." Bern spun around in the middle of his song. "What?"

I dropped my voice like I did when I was in the booth. "You're listening to K-T-*Essss*-Y, home of soft and classic rock. Now, for your auditory enjoyment, here's a little Led Zeppelin from our house to yours. Turn us up or turn us down, but definitely keep us tuuuuurned on."

Navy folded into laughter. "You do not have to say that!"

I nodded. "All the time."

"Say it again," Bern demanded, with a huge grin.

"Turn us up or turn us down, but definitely keep us tuuuuurned on." I drawled it out a little longer this time, in my deep, I'm-not-seventeen voice.

Bern laughed. "That's brilliant!"

"Late night?" Isaiah asked.

"It's the only spot they give the newbies, fewest listeners and all that. Can't mess up too bad, and if you do, there's not really anyone to care."

"Your parents let you do that?" Navy asked.

"My parents get having a passion." For a thing, anyway, just not for each other.

She ran her fingers along a delicate gold necklace with a figure eight attached at the center of the chain. Like I was being sized up, or deemed interesting, and my palms went sweaty.

"Is that what you want to do with your life?" she asked. "Be

21

a DJ?"

"Yes." I cleared my throat. "However, I'm the only heir to an industrious family business."

"Which is?"

"A tattoo shop." I watched her closely, but she didn't flinch.

"Your dad start it?" Isaiah asked, which was a total judgment, not that I could blame him. My dad was pretty covered.

"My mom's dad actually. But my dad works there." Although I guess that might be awkward under the circumstances. Would he lose his job? Would he leave?

You and dad work together, I'd pointed out in another message. *You're going to have to face us sooner or later. Just please answer your phone, and we can fix this,* I'd begged, because Lord knew Dad wouldn't, even if he wanted to.

I'll leave soup in the fridge for when you get home, okay?

"What about your mom?" Navy asked.

My mouth went to cotton when I tried to say it. But who cared what I told these people? I'd only know them for a week. "She's, um, she works for the cruise line actually."

"Like, she's working on the ship?" Bern asked.

"Nah, she's in the Caribbean right now. Six months on and six months off. We've already done that a million times, though, so she surprised us with Alaska instead."

She'd surprised us all right. That part was the damn truth.

Navy

It was miserable watching Jesse's smile wilt and slip off his face. Something about his mom, but then, I knew what moms could be like. One day laughing and relaxed, playing card games until our eyes went numb, then the next dressed to the nines and wrapped in fake, all to impress a man.

Jesse was a contradiction too, but in a better way: smiles, rosy cheeks, and buoyant dark curls against stormy blue eyes and tattoos.

I wanted my first kiss to be special, but maybe the guy seeming perfect was enough, if I never knew any better. I mean, unless I wanted to be an unkissed seventeen-year-old, it was now or never. I wouldn't meet anyone in Kansas City until school started, well after my birthday.

I gazed out the window to get away from it, from the fact that I'd made him uncomfortable. The sea stretched far until it met mountains, and the light was fading, blurring the scenery and waves into a splotchy inkblot against the lighter sky.

"What about you, Midnight?" Bern asked. "You have a job?"

"No. Too busy moving all the time."

"What does that mean?" Jesse asked.

"It means my mom gets bored." I fiddled with the thin ring on my pointer finger. Bored with the men, the gossip, or people gossiping about her, I could never tell. Or maybe she was still running from my dad's ghost. "I guess you could call us gypsies." Travelers, whose entire belongings fit in a car. Nomads, with no actual location to call home.

"ATTENTION PASSENGERS: PLEASE NOTE THAT THERE IS A LOST AND FOUND AT THE PASSENGER SERVICES DESK ON DECK SIX. IF YOU FOUND ANYTHING TODAY THAT DOES NOT BELONG TO YOU, WE ASK THAT YOU HEAD TO THE PASSENGER SERVICES DESK IMMEDIATELY AND NO CHARGES WILL BE FILED."

Jesse cocked his head to the ceiling. "That's weird."

"Yeah," Bern drew the sound out as he picked another song on the video game. "Like something was stolen?"

Jesse scanned the room for the nearest coordinator, who wasn't coordinating all that much at the moment. "I'll ask," he said, making his way around a handful of people standing awkwardly in a circle.

The coordinator was in college probably, and smiling so wide as Jesse walked up to her that it was possible she was missing a few brain cells. I frowned as they fell into a deep discussion.

"He's charming, huh?" Bern grinned.

"I'm charming," Isaiah muttered, crossing his arms and catching my eye.

Bern let out a short chuckle. "Oh, don't worry, Cowboy. That you are." Then he went back to the game. When his turn was over, he yelled for Jesse to hurry. Jesse held up a finger, his head still bent down toward the girl's. Her face was going to freeze that way if she didn't knock it off.

Jesse finally ran over to jump in on the second few beats, and while he danced, he shared: "That's Toni . . . She has a buddy in security . . . Some lady thinks her purse was stolen in line . . . boarding . . . while her husband had it . . . Husband swears he wouldn't lose his wife's purse . . . also swears he wouldn't leave it somewhere." He finished with a spin and turned to face us on the couch. His shorts hung low on his hips, and his hair was fluffed from the movement.

I smiled. Isaiah tapped his foot, which caused the cowboy boot propped on his knee to tap into me. Readjusting, I folded my legs the other way and checked that I had the appropriate amount of empty space around me in all directions.

Toni didn't seem to have a problem with personal space. Or smiles. She was still smiling at Jesse from across the room, and he wasn't even looking at her.

He was looking at me. I straightened up.

"Toni also said they're showing a movie later. Who's game?"

I could already feel it in my stomach, the time change. Or maybe that was from the barely there vibrations of the boat. *A highly sensitive person,* my mom always said with a wave of her hand, sometimes even a roll of her eyes. And the thought of how every little thing affected me had my stomach twisting tighter. "No thanks, I crash early."

"Up with the dawn, down with the dusk," Isaiah said with a lazy grin in my direction. "Internal clock won't have it any other way."

"Are you guys teenagers?" Bern asked. "What kind of baloney is that?"

"I've been on the ranch for awhile now," Isaiah said. "Can't help it anymore."

Bern lifted his palms to the air. "And he is an actual cowboy!"

"You live on a ranch?" I asked.

"Most of the year."

"Mmm," Bern sighed. "Tell us about it."

"Mostly it's shoveling horseshit and leading trail rides, but we guide hunts too."

"Like, deer hunts?" Jesse asked.

"No. Elk and bear."

"You hunt bear?" Bern raised a perfect eyebrow.

"Yeah. In the backcountry. Four weeks under the stars," Isaiah said wistfully, like he already missed it.

This guy was hard-core. First kiss with a rugged cowboy? Not something easily forgotten, I'd give him that.

"What about school?" Jesse asked.

"Says the late night radio DJ," Bern muttered behind his hand.

"Dude, I get up for school."

"I just went the summers in the beginning, then got my GED when I was old enough for the hunting."

No wonder he seemed so mature. "Your parents were okay

with that?"

He shrugged. "The ranch was all I could think about, so Gram made me a deal."

"Why was it all you could think about?" I asked. It had to be about more than horses. You could find horses anywhere.

He grimaced too, like I was right, and like I'd poked too far. Glancing over at Jesse and Bern, I stood up. "Since we both go to bed early, will you walk me back to the rooms?"

"Of course."

"Hey," Jesse said. "How are we going to find each other tomorrow?"

Pulling out my phone, I went to enter a new contact. After reciting his number, he added, "But I'm not supposed to use my phone. My dad says it's too expensive, the Wi-Fi and out of country charges. International sea and all that." Isaiah and Bern started in on their cells, and Jesse reluctantly reached for his. "Can't we meet here or something?"

"How about eight o'clock at the buffet," Isaiah suggested.

"Eight o'clock?" Bern snorted, while Jesse scrunched his shoulders and pretended to be walking with a cane.

I laughed. "We're planning on room service. The deck and sea and coffee with a view? Delightful." Or at least, delightful was what my mom had promised.

And there went Jesse again, a hunched-back old man muttering "delightful" over and over. Bern pretended to wrap a shawl around his shoulders, and I planted my hands on my hips, even though I was laughing.

Jesse straightened and tossed me a semi-apologetic expression, like he was hoping it entertained me and I hadn't taken it the wrong way. I hadn't. I grinned at him.

"I'll be at the buffet at noon for my breakfast, your lunch," Jesse said. "Text me if there's an emergency before that."

"An emergency?" Isaiah repeated.

"Yeah, like you stumbled on the jewel thief or something."

"Pickpocket, Messy. So far, it's just a pickpocket."

Jesse shoved Bern lightly, like they'd known each other forever. "Let's go make some popcorn." Jesse said. "Toni told me where to find it."

Isaiah

"I'm on the Dauphin deck," Navy said as we stepped into the hall. "You?"

I nodded, even though it was a lie. Aunt Ethel was on the Dauphin deck. Gram and I were one level up in a stuffy interior room.

"So." Navy punched the elevator's down button and twisted her hair over one shoulder. "Why was the ranch all you could think about? And where were your parents when you got your GED?"

"That's why you wanted to get me alone?"

"We only have a week." Letting go of her hair, she crossed

her arms. "Might as well skip the small talk."

I stared at her.

She studied my silence for one second. Then took a deep breath. "Listen," she said. "My dad died when I was a baby. If I were old enough to remember any of it, I'd share it with you right now. As it is, my mom's dragged me around the country ever since, never getting close to Georgia because that's where he was from—where they were from. Anyway, point is, she avoids the Deep South because of losing him, but I've never gotten that. I've always figured, if it were me, I'd want to go back, to feel him everywhere in the way people talk and the food she goes on about him making. So it seems possible to me that perhaps your parents were part of that ranch, and they died, and you couldn't think about anything but going back."

"This is your way of asking me if my parents died?"

"I feel an affinity towards people who've also lost their parents." She sighed. "It's okay if you don't."

The elevator opened, and we stepped in.

"Come on, Isaiah." She surveyed the space between us. Took a small step closer. "Tell me and in a week I'll be gone, like I never existed, and you never spilled your deepest darkests."

All night she'd been avoiding contact, leaning away. Now she was inching closer. If she swung her hair out hard enough, it might even brush my arm. I made a fist to keep my fingers in check. "We went every summer, for vacation," I admitted. "My dad and I."

Navy straightened, a smile growing that wiped out every bit of nasty her face implied without it.

My heart galloped in my chest. *Keep talking, Isaiah, keep it up. This is the way to get your hands on her hair and your ranch back. Focus.*

"I'm sure I'll be off to Harvard soon, though. I've got all this money from my parents. Gotta put it to good use." Yeah, right. All my parents left me was my grandma.

Ranch hands didn't make much money. It was a way of life. But so far Jesse had pulled more smiles from Navy than I had. If a Harvard lie got me the girl, well, I only had to keep up the charade for a week.

"I'm going to Georgia for college." She clipped her syllables, as if this usually started an argument.

"Because of your dad?" I asked.

She nodded. I reached out to squeeze her hand. Then let go right away so it wasn't awkward. Just because I was quiet didn't mean I wasn't tuned in to others. You read horses long enough, you learn to read energy.

Wiping her palm on her pants as we stepped out of the elevator, Navy looked both ways. I'd been doing this too. It took a second to orient yourself to which side of the ship was which.

After a few more glances, she led me left. Then hung a right into the long corridor. This deck only had rooms on the outside, all of them opening on the ocean. Her suite would be as fancy as Aunt Ethel's.

"I think we're in the wrong hall," she finally said, swinging back through the elevator space. On the other side of the ship, she hustled down to the last door.

"This is me," she announced. "Where are you?"

I checked the wall for arrows pointing in the direction of Ethel's room. "The other end."

"I'll look for you in the morning after breakfast," she said with a smile. "I'm glad they sat us with you guys."

I tipped my hat. "I'm glad they sat me with you."

Day 2: At sea

Navy

"That Wally Kowalski. He could drink you under the table, Guy." My mom sipped her coffee, leaving a lipstick stain on the rim. Seven in the morning, and she'd already applied.

"That he could, Delilah. That he could." Guy was the perfect audience for Mom's gossip, keeping her fueled with a few absent comments and agreeable smiles.

"I don't think his name is actually Wally Kowalski," I told her. "He said 'they call me Wally,' not 'I'm Wally.' Get it?" But they only stared at me. "I think they call him Wally because his name is Ko*wal*ski."

"Three drinks for dinner." My mom held up the heavy fingers of her right hand. "Then straight to the bar after. I bet he's in bed till two, bless his heart."

"That Jesse seems like a nice kid, though," Guy said. He was in his pajamas like I was, and we were huddled on our deck in blankets, because even though it was June, out on the water it was nearly frigid. My scrambled eggs had dropped from steaming to clammy in the five minutes it took me to eat them, but it was worth it. Fact was, we were eating breakfast with a first row seat to the middle of the ocean.

Okay, not middle, but it felt like it.

"He's cute, but he might be trouble," my mom said. "Be careful with that one, hear?"

"Because of his dad?" I asked. "Maybe he has a good reason."

"Everyone has a good reason," Guy agreed. "A person can still choose not to."

"You saying you'd have good reason to drink instead of eat?" I asked.

"Not anymore." He winked at me. "Not with your mom around."

She leaned over for a quick peck, her hand jumping to tousle his gray streaked hair. Gross. At least they kept their tongues in check when I was watching.

"You can't judge a kid by his parent," I said.

"Ooh, you think Jesse's cute, don't you baby?"

"Mom. The point is—"

"The point is you don't want people assuming you're like your mother?" She was smiling, teasing. Though, she wasn't wrong either. "Classy and well-bred? I hate to tell you, doll, but even with that inconspicuous uniform you so like, you still come off that way."

My jeans and white tees had long been a note of contention, as well as the designer clothes—staple pieces—she'd insisted on buying for me that took up too much space in our car on moving days.

"Don't be getting into trouble, all right?" Guy was the king of diversions. Sometimes I didn't mind him much because of it.

"What trouble could I possibly get into on this ship?"

"Trouble follows trouble," Guy said. "If that boy's trouble, he'll find it."

"He's not trouble. He's a late night radio DJ. That's like a real job, and he's still in high school."

"Late night?" Mom arched one of her salon-styled eyebrows. "When does he sleep?"

I rolled my eyes. She thought enough sleep would cure anything.

"He's probably one of those kids who doesn't go to school because they sleep in and their parents don't care. Where's his mother?"

"She works for the cruise line," I told her. "Six months on and six months off." With my final bite of eggs, I slid inside to peek down the hall. I'd been keeping an eye out for Isaiah since I woke up, not that I was ready to spend the whole morning with him, alone. But then, it was thoughts like that which led to why I hadn't yet been kissed.

"What's out there?" my mom asked, when I came back with more blankets.

"Isaiah's down the hall, but if he's not up yet, I don't want to wake him." Though, he had said up with the dawn.

"He's cute too. You hit the jackpot, Navy girl." My mom reached a hand out for my chin and made me look at her. "Which one will it be?" And she puckered her lips at the same time she forced me to pucker mine.

I wrenched away and reminded her, "It's too soon to tell."

Jesse

My foot wouldn't stop shaking, that's how much I wanted to see her again.

Or maybe it was the energy of the ship, the incessant chatter from the swarm of people, most moving with purpose and all propelled by wonder. There was a lot of pointing, I'd noticed. *Look at this! Look at that!*

So at least I wasn't the only one.

It was a little after noon, and I'd stopped circling the large café five minutes ago. If I stayed put, then she—they—were bound to find me. Four minutes and I'd let myself text her. Hopefully Dad wouldn't notice, now that he'd so easily found his way into a booze bottle.

Thanks for that, Mom.

I could only pray Navy wasn't the type to ditch me, but if my

35

own mother would do it, who wouldn't?

"Boo!"

Startled, I spun in my seat to find her smiling at me. Fresh white tee and new feather earrings, but the same dark skinny jeans and sandals with the straps running every which way. Same gold necklace, and same glossy, unbeatable lips.

I sighed. Sweet, sweet distraction. "Good morning."

"Good afternoon." She grinned. "Feel like shopping?"

"Sure. After lunch."

Sliding into the seat next to me, she muttered, "Oh, I suppose." But it was a teasing mutter. "We wait for Bern and Isaiah before we grab anything?"

"Or we take turns," I suggested.

"You that hungry? Didn't you have popcorn with Toni?"

Studying her slightly pursed lips and furrowed brow, I decided on, "We fed each other too."

She laughed and swatted at me. Then, probably due to the serious look on my face—because I seriously loved her laughing—she quieted. "You're serious?"

"No, I'm not serious! You think I'd bed an informant?"

She snickered. "Yes, I think you would do whatever it takes."

If only there was something I could do about uncooperative radio silence, which is all I was getting from my mother. "Some of us have morals, Navy. I would do nothing to compromise the case."

With a doubtful grin, she leaned back in her chair and brightened at whoever was behind me. Bern, I could tell from the cologne that preceded him, placed his palms on my shoulders and gave a little squeeze.

"Mmmhmm." Navy crossed her arms. "I see who you fed your popcorn to."

Wait, was she jealous?

Bern circled around and squeezed her shoulders too. She stiffened. Was that because of Isaiah walking toward us? Had something happened with them on the way to their rooms last night?

Damn, he really did have that cowboy edge down.

"Rugged perfection," Bern muttered, and I couldn't exactly disagree. Sandwiched between the dark cowboy hat and lighter cowboy boots was a whole lot of muscle. I ran my hands along my biceps and sighed.

I was no competition. In fact, I was futile. Handcuffed by the sea, international roaming charges, and a father who refused to try and save us.

Navy

While we ate, we moved from table to table, closer and closer to the windows as the lunch crowd cleared. I was watching the sea roll toward the mountains in the distance and listening to Jesse and Bern argue about their favorite football teams when

Toni appeared.

Her hair was pulled half back with skinny braids scattered randomly about her head, very bohemian disheveled. A person only looked that messy if they were trying to make it look like they didn't care.

Jesse formally introduced her to Isaiah and me, since we'd left early last night, and she took Isaiah's hand with both of hers, her smile nearly splitting her face. Distracted by the chain wrapping her wrist and the multicolored pattern of polish on her nails, I missed my moment to avoid a handshake. Or whatever she called this two on one thing she was doing.

"Nice to meet you, Navy! You guys should've stayed last night! Tonight, for sure, we have lots of cool stuff planned!" A double-handed squeeze, long and what she clearly wanted me to think was sincere. But I wasn't going to trust someone who put so much work into the expression on their face.

Jerking away, I slid finger by finger through the napkin in my lap, wiping my hands as best I could. If only I hadn't forgotten to move my hand sanitizer from my backpack to my purse. The ship had stations everywhere but bolting for one would be rude.

She settled in the chair on the other side of Jesse, as if someone had invited her to sit down, and smoothed her shirt like my mom did when there was a reasonably attractive man around. Toni had to be significantly older than us though, and it was skeezy to hit on someone in your charge, which we technically were.

"How old do you have to be to babysit on this boat?" I asked, my face smooth and innocent.

"Twenty-one." Both of her hands were working one braid, twirling it around like a girl in middle school. "But I think of it as coordinating."

"Whatever it is, you do a great job," Jesse said.

"Aw, thanks! I think you're pretty great up there too. Some people aren't good about participating. Wet blankets take a real toll on our vibe, you know?"

Isaiah snorted. "Maybe they aren't wet blankets. Maybe they just think organized activities are stupid."

"Thank you," I said sincerely.

He tipped his hat at me. "You're very welcome."

The slightest pout flashed across Toni's perpetually upbeat face, and Jesse asked, "Have you ever wondered what that really means? *You're welcome?*"

I smiled. "I have actually."

"What are you talking about?" Bern asked.

"You are welcome," Jesse said, drawing the words out. "You are more than welcome. Welcome tripped me up when I started thinking about it. Like, welcome is a greeting, a motion to come inside someone's house or something."

"Right." I grinned. "So you're saying 'you're more than welcome to thank me, do it again, I know I'm so awesome I deserve thanks.'"

Jesse leaned forward. "Exactly."

"Did you know that in French, it's *'de rien'*, and *rien* means nothing. So they say, like, 'oh, it's nothing.' Or they say *'Je vous en prie'* which translates to 'don't mention it' or 'I'm pleased to do it for you,' which is maybe what we think we're saying, but really, we're saying, 'please, thank me again.'"

"I didn't mean you should thank me again," Isaiah said.

"I know." I glanced at him with a reassuring smile.

"I always thought of it like 'You're welcome to it'," Toni said. Of course she did. "Anyway, you guys coming up after lunch?" But it was clear this question was for Jesse alone, as her irritatingly easy grin sprouted in his direction. I pulled the strap of my purse off the back of the chair and flung it over my shoulder. If she was staying, I was going. And hopefully taking Jesse with me. I looked at him.

Jesse caught my eye and answered, "Nah, I think my girl here wants to shop."

"Oh!" She looked back and forth between us. "You two are together?"

"No, I mean like, not *my* girl, just, you know, this girl." His face bloomed red as we both stared at him. "We, um, only met yesterday."

"Just like you two," I added, turning on Toni with an innocent smile. See, I could fake happiness too. Then I spun for the elevator.

The three of them said goodbye to her in their various

ways, then came up beside me as the door dinged open. After we'd stepped in, Jesse said, "You don't like her, huh?"

"She smiles too much," Isaiah answered. "And what's with all the enthusiasm?"

I kept my mouth shut, not that I disagreed.

"Maybe she's just that happy," Jesse offered.

When the elevator doors reopened, Bern led the way through a lounge where an art auction was going on. Guy and Ethel were in the front row. He was perched on a chair while she stood next to him, holding a paddle. Mom and Isaiah's grandma were in the seats directly behind them, chattering to each other.

Guy and his art. Who needed more stuff to lug around from move to move? No one, that's who.

As we exited the lounge, the hall opened up wider. It was lined with display after display of the photos we'd taken on the deck, right before we'd boarded the ship. I slowed down when I saw ours.

Jesse and Bern wandered off to look for theirs, and Isaiah peered over my shoulder. "Nice picture."

Guy's arm was around my mom, her palm propped on his bicep. My hip was stuck out, my arms crossed, and, as I noted out loud, "That's my bitchy resting face." I definitely didn't agree with him that it was nice.

"That's what you call it?" he asked.

Dimples popped up on his cheeks when he talked. They

made me want to keep him talking. "That's what it is."

"I like it."

"You like my bitchy resting face?"

He nodded, pointing to the picture. "Your hair looks great too."

I grinned, tossing said hair over my shoulder and readjusting my purse. Except, suddenly it didn't feel like my purse. Grabbing it with both hands, I looked down and confirmed.

Somehow, somewhere, I'd left my purse and taken someone else's.

Isaiah

Navy was having a panic attack. I'd never seen one before but wasn't sure what else could be happening.

I reached a hand out for her shoulder, then changed my mind. She was jumpy about space. Even in one day I had that figured. "Asthma?"

Gasping for words, she shook her head.

"Do you need a medic?"

She shook it harder but her face was draining of color.

"Are you sure?" I pulled my cell out. "What's 911 on this boat?"

"No." She clutched my wrist. "Don't."

Bern loped over. "Hey, you okay?" He looked to me and my

arm, where she was digging neat and no-nonsense fingernails into my skin. I shook free. "What'd you do?" he asked.

"Nothing! I didn't do anything." I put my hands in the air. "She's having a panic attack or something."

Jesse, a few beats behind Bern, slid his hand across her back and ran it in circles. "Breathe, Navy. It's okay. Think of something else, anything. Think of home, or, I guess, your favorite home. A safe place anyway. What did it look like, what was your favorite thing there?"

She shook her head. "I'm not having a panic attack. I just. You guys!"

"What?" If this wasn't for real, then why all the drama?

Her purse fell off her shoulder, and she took a step away from it. "That's not my purse!"

"You stole someone's purse?" I asked.

"You think she'd be freaking out if she did it on purpose?" Jesse snapped. Then, to her. "It was a mistake. We'll figure it out."

She gaped at him. "They're going to think I took it. And the other one. They're going to think *I'm* the thief." She choked on the last word and leaned against him. The girl with space issues and an addiction to hand sanitizer—she stopped at every single station—was falling into Jesse, hair all over him.

"They might," I agreed, wondering if we were dealing with some great mastermind here. Honestly, a thief might be easier to take than a drama queen.

"Yeah, I don't want to be in the middle of this," Bern said, taking a few steps back. "Plus, my dad wanted the fam to play Bingo this afternoon. I'll catch you guys later."

We stared at him. He looked to be waiting for permission. No one gave it. A few more steps back, and he spun to hustle away.

"That's helpful," Jesse muttered, picking the purse up off the ground.

Navy grabbed it from him. "You carrying it is even more suspicious. I'll bring it in."

"Before we bring it in," Jesse said, "we're going back up to see if anyone is looking for it. See if yours is still there. Honest mix-up, swap back, all taken care of."

"That sounds like a plan A," I said. "Plan As are plan As because you end up needing the plan B."

They frowned at me. But if there was one thing I'd learned, it was that things were never as easy as a simple plan A.

Jesse

Her purse was strapped across the chair of the third table we'd been at. The imposter—same length, same color, same shape, only with a different fabric on the flap—must have been left behind too. Flinging them both over her shoulder, Navy dug for a Kleenex in what I was going to hope was her own purse and blew her nose.

We spent half an hour wandering the buffet's extended dining room, but no one looked like they were searching for anything. No easy plan A, as Isaiah had predicted.

Navy slumped in a chair.

"Leave it at the last table we were at," Isaiah said.

"But which one was our last table?"

Isaiah and I immediately pointed in opposite directions, both so sure we hadn't even had to think about it.

With a moan, Navy ran her hands over her face. "Exactly! And everything's identical on the other side of the boat, which means how do we know we weren't over there?"

Table after table after table after table, windows and buffets situated in exactly the same spot on both sides, it was a lime and coral Rorschach inkblot. Mirror images that made you feel like you'd fallen into a 4D maze and couldn't tell which way was up.

"Just leave it," Isaiah said. "Someone will find it."

"Or someone will steal it," she countered. "And then that will be our fault."

"We're not going to leave it," I said. "When you find something that's not yours, you turn it in. Just because a purse has already been stolen on board doesn't mean we don't do the right thing."

"I was never planning on doing the wrong thing!" she cried.

Isaiah raised an eyebrow at me. Even though we barely knew each other, I read him loud and clear: *does the lady protest too much?*

Disgusted with him, I slid into the seat next to her and gave her my steadiest, surest gaze. "I know." When she looked in my eyes, the connection felt physical, like we were holding hands.

"But are they going to think I stole it?" she asked, her voice quiet.

"Of course not," I answered, but not loudly enough to counter Isaiah's obvious shrug.

The three of us were silent for a minute, Navy and I in chairs and Isaiah standing like a marble statue. Silence wasn't helping, and waiting wasn't helping. Navy kept peeking at the purse out of the corner of her eye, and her clasped fingers, though she must have been trying to hold them down, were shaking.

"Give it to me," I said, with an unintended boom of bravado in my voice. Clearing my throat to get rid of it, I tried again, "I'll take care of it. I'll get it to Toni."

"That's stupid," Navy snapped. "She'll just think you like her."

"Is that so bad, under the circumstances?" An employee could easily sneak it to lost and found without suspicion.

Isaiah grunted. "If you're going to turn it in, you should bring it to passenger services like they said in the announcement."

Navy stood, holding tight to both straps, and looked toward the elevator with rounded eyes and tight lips.

But really, it didn't have to be her. The thief from yesterday didn't return the purse, and the fact that we were made the difference. If there had been no announcement last night, we wouldn't think anything of bringing a purse to lost and found, and the way we were sitting here, the way her hands were shaking, was only making her seem more guilty.

She couldn't be the one to do it.

I grabbed the purse from her and marched to the elevator. They could come with me or not, it didn't matter. I was just bringing something to lost and found. The good guy. The hero. Maybe Mom would come home if a hero was waiting for her.

Winding the strap around the small clutch, I tucked it tight into my chest as the elevator opened on a security officer.

Navy

I noticed the guy's badge immediately, and a lifetime's worth of shame plugged up my throat.

My dad was surely turning in his grave. Not a shadow, not a cloud, not a hint of doubt would touch me. That was supposed to be my legacy for the sake of the father I'd never known. And now here I was, guilty by association. Guilty by accident.

The officer zoomed in on it, hidden under Jesse's arm. That did look a little shady, actually, and being he was still frozen, not offering it up or taking a step back looked even worse.

"That your purse?" he asked in a thick French accent.

"No, it's not his purse," I answered, as the doors began to close. He slammed his hand on the button to keep them open and narrowed his eyes at me. I tugged Jesse back by his shirt to give him room to step out. "We were just on our way to the lost and found."

Jesse put his hand out. "Nice to meet you . . . ?"

The Frenchman didn't move. "Benoît."

"Benoît! Benny! Perfect!" Jesse dropped his head back in relief. "Toni was talking about you last night, man. She'll vouch for us."

"Benoît. Not Benny." He crossed his arms. "How long have you known Toni?"

Jesse's smile died. He went still again and cleared his throat. "Since yesterday."

Benoît snorted and slipped a hand through the crook of Jesse's elbow.

"Where're we going?" Jesse asked. "Lost and found?"

"Questioning. You are to be questioned."

"He's innocent!" I cried. "He has witnesses!"

"You are one person."

I spun to Isaiah, who was hanging back ten feet. A glare from me, and he stepped forward.

Benoît's gaze shot back and forth between the two of us. "And how long have you known the suspect?"

"Depuis hier," I answered, as Isaiah said, "Yesterday." Exactly. And my French worked too. Benoît's shoulders

relaxed, a smile tugged at the corner of his lips, and he let go of Jesse.

In different circumstances, I would've followed this Frenchman around and asked him for some organic translations, the kind you could only know from actually living somewhere.

Standing taller, I linked my arm through Jesse's. "We really were on our way to lost and found, so if you're taking him, you're taking me."

Isaiah stepped up next to me. "We ate, hopped a few tables to get the good view, ended up at one that had a purse at it. We waited, no one came. Jesse here was taking matters into his own hands."

My jaw clenched. That was not the truth.

Benoît raised an eyebrow. "The owner of the item searched the area."

"Not good enough," Isaiah said, without missing a beat. Maybe that was the key to lying, thinking fast and not missing a beat.

"Where were you sitting?"

Isaiah pointed in the same direction he'd pointed last time, and I hoped his sense of direction was better than Jesse's. It should be, right? He was a cowboy.

Benoît's grin was smug. "She said she was on the other side of the boat."

I glared at Isaiah and stepped forward. "We ate, hopped a

few tables to get the good view, then left. We were gone maybe five minutes when I realized I had the wrong purse. That was probably when they were searching the area. Look, see how similar they are?" I offered up my purse, still slung around my shoulder. He glanced at it. Dropping it back to my side, I continued. "Anyway, I panicked, obviously, so we came back, found my purse, and didn't want to leave this one in case someone stole it, you know?"

"So two witnesses with two different stories, and you saying it was your fault when he's the one with the purse." Benoît narrowed his eyes at Jesse. "You have anything to add, Suspect Number One?"

"I'm with Navy. That's the truth." Jesse shoved the purse at Benoît, who opened the flap, unzipped it, and rifled through. Pulling out a wallet, he flipped it open and peered into the billfold.

He looked back up at Jesse. "Then tell me where this lady's two hundred dollars went."

Isaiah

Had someone stolen cash out of the purse before we sat down next to it? Or was someone putting on a show?

"I was with him the whole time, sir." Navy held her chin high. "He did *not* open that purse."

"That's true," I added. It was the least I could do.

Benoît burst out with a laugh, slapping his leg with amusement. Weird guffaws echoed through the huge space.

Clapping a hand on Jesse's shoulder, he snickered. "Nothing missing. Just nice to break things up with some laughs." He tucked the purse deep in his armpit and grabbed a pad of paper and pencil out of his pocket. "Lucky you have witnesses, or we'd be down in the pit talking it out. For now, I'll take your info." He flipped through his small notepad and found a blank page. "And if we run into each other again under like circumstances,"—he looked up with a serious face, a serious warning—"I will find you, interrogate you, search your room, you name it. Two strikes and you're out, understand?"

We passed the pad around, wrote our numbers in it. He was still chuckling when he left.

Navy crumpled into a chair. Jesse felt backward until he found one of his own.

"Shit," he muttered.

"That was close," Navy agreed.

"It wasn't close." Seriously, these two with the drama. "You didn't do anything wrong."

"He was testing us," Jesse said.

Navy groaned. "My mom always did say I was piss poor at lying."

Jesse snorted. "My mom too."

"My mom always told me I better learn how to do it well."

Navy squinted at me. "That's awful."

I shrugged. My mom was a good lady. It was the situation that couldn't be helped.

"Now what?" Jesse asked.

"We were going shopping."

"Ugh," Navy groaned. "After that I don't think I'm in the mood."

"Probably safest in the teen lounge," Jesse agreed.

She snorted more than laughed, then pulled her phone out of her pocket. "That is not what I'm saying." After checking her messages, she looked to Jesse. "My mom saw your dad at the piazza bar. She thinks you should check on him."

Jesse

The piazza was a dramatic drop of three stories, from gigantic chandelier to marble-tiled floor, all of it amped up with sparkling lights, sweeping staircases, and curlicue railings shaded in mahogany, gold, and marble.

The bottom level had seating and dessert cafés, then two tiers of shops, and the piano bar up top. My dad was slumped over next to a ray of sunlight, an empty glass next to him.

"Dad," I hissed. Navy and Isaiah were maybe twenty feet behind me, tentative and waiting, and I was definitely embarrassed—by the state of my father, the state of my family, that Navy and Isaiah were seeing this, and that it was even happening.

"How many drinks have you had?" I pressed, leaning closer.

"Not enough." He pulled himself up, shoulders hunched and eyes squinty, but he still didn't look at me. Rather, he focused on the bottles lined haphazardly inside the glass cabinet against the back wall, as if he was calculating how long it would take to go through each and every one.

Glancing back at Navy and Isaiah, I set a hand on the bar and leaned into it, trying to block him from their view. I mean, did she have to look so concerned? The last thing I wanted was for her to pity me.

"Why are you doing this?"

"Why do you think?" He waved me off.

My dad was a complicated guy, but he'd tried. I'd watched him try. I'd listened to him tell me to be better than he was. He'd told me to do what he said and not what he did, because you couldn't teach an old dog new tricks, but you could teach a puppy better.

So he could be sexist and rude, but he brought flowers and chocolates and poems even, when he was trying to be who he wanted me to be. So he was gruff, but he was gentle and generous too.

I swallowed. "You look . . ." He looked like shit, reinforcing the stereotypes he'd spent his life fighting.

"I don't care how I look. I'll never see these people again."

"You'll see them tonight, Dad. And tomorrow." I ran a hand through my hair, tugging at the ends. "This isn't you. What are you doing?"

"I'm doing what I need to do, Jess. Now you do what you need to do."

But that was the thing: what I needed was to save my family, only my parents weren't cooperating. I also, as of twenty minutes ago when I inadvertently made it onto Benoît's radar, needed to not look like a thief, or like I came from a family of questionable origin.

"I think we should get you back to the room for a nap."

"Don't make this worse by trying to take care of me."

Dropping my arms to my sides, I studied him—the stubble, the wife-beater, the suspenders with one clip skewed. I redid it, wondering why he hadn't bothered to add a nice button-down to the ensemble like usual. He had any number of crisp, collared shirts hanging in our room.

Batting me away, he grunted. "That's what I mean by making it worse."

"Making what worse?" There wasn't anything that could make this worse, if you asked me.

"My humiliation," he muttered.

I slid onto the seat next to him. "Have you talked to her?"

Running a hand over his face, he groaned. "Go enjoy yourself. That's what would help this trip not be a total waste."

Unsure whether or not I could leave him, I dared another look at Navy and Isaiah. She rushed up as if I'd asked for help, and I shook my head but it was too late. Leaning close to my ear, heat brushing my lobe, she whispered quietly, "If we shop, we can keep an eye on him from down there."

We were near enough the balcony that I could see the store two levels down and across the way, but no, I couldn't leave him. Maybe if I stayed, it would slow him down, conscience and all that. So I slid onto the stool for good.

Turning back to Navy, I did my best to hide my angst and aimed for apologetic. "I'll see you at dinner?"

She frowned, but somehow it felt the same as a sympathetic smile. There was no pity in it, something more reassuring than that, and she squeezed my shoulder before turning for Isaiah. They took to the grand staircase, and I watched as they wandered along the rail the level below us until finally disappearing into a clothing store.

Navy

"Baby, get this." My mom paused to apply her Peach Perfect lipstick in our living room mirror. Guy was in the shower, and I was putting on heels for the ship's first formal dinner. "That Isaiah? He's gay." She nodded at her reflection and recapped the tube. "Guess that leaves you with Jesse or that other hot catch we saw you walking by the art auction with."

"That other hot catch is definitely gay." I adjusted my dress. "But Isaiah isn't."

She set a palm over her heart. "Straight from his Gram's

lips."

I eyed her, knowing exactly how untrue something from a gossiper's mouth could be. "What exactly did she say?"

"Said he likes that ranch because of all the boys, but she won't let him go back and be miserable the rest of his life."

"If he loves the ranch, why would he be miserable?"

"His daddy struggled with depression, and she thinks if he holes himself up in the middle of nowhere without a family, that the same thing's going to happen to him."

"He told me he's going to Harvard next year." I reached for my lip gloss, but Mom stilled my hand and grabbed her tube, wiping the tip off with a tissue. She opened her mouth to prompt me to do the same, so I did.

While she painstakingly applied it for me, she babbled on. "Liza didn't mention college. In fact, she said he has no ambition, and she doesn't know what to do with him. He doesn't care if he makes nothing, but what about when she's gone and he wants to support a family? I said, maybe he doesn't want a family. Maybe the boys and horses are enough for him."

"And the bears," I added, as she finished. She gave me a look. "He bear hunts too. And elk. I don't think he's gay." Granted, I wasn't the best judge of who was flirting with me or not, but last night in the hall, I'd sworn he was looking at me like he was completely hetero.

The water shut off in the bathroom, and she leaned toward

me with a whisper. "Ethel's sort of a loose one too, bless her heart. Liza says she's opened her legs for as many men as she is years old." My mom tsked, and I was sure my face reflected the vomit threatening my esophagus.

"Enough, Mom, okay?" She turned so I could clasp her dress, then we swapped, and she did the same for me. "You don't know how true any of that is."

"If she doesn't know, then who does?" Standing face-to-face, she reached behind me to separate my hair into two chunks, then rested it in front of my shoulders, adjusted my necklace, and fiddled with my sleeves.

"Do not be spreading rumors about these people," I warned. "It's only day two."

She patted my cheek, an official approval of my readiness, as Guy opened the bathroom door. He was hidden by a partition and another open doorway, but was probably dressing by the closet. And since he was a little too open with his naked body for my comfort, I headed to my bedroom. He might have thought we were close enough to father/daughter not to worry about it, but I was sixteen and he was not my daddy.

Fingering my loosely curled hair, I wondered about Isaiah. Fact was, he was a man compared to all the boys I'd known before, layered and built up from the rough years he'd spent on that ranch. Fine, if he was gay, but I couldn't see it. Wouldn't he be all over Bern then? Because my mom was right, Bern was a hot catch.

Isaiah

"I'm sorry, what?"

"Sir, you cannot eat this evening, dressed like that. You must be in formal attire."

Aunt Ethel shook her fluffed-up head. "I told you, Liza."

"I *work* for a living," I told the guy. "This is the first time I've needed anything but work clothes."

"Since his parents' funeral," Gram added with a huff. "And that was twelve inches ago, so this is as good as he's got. You know, funerals are supposed to be formal attire too, but you see all sorts a people comin' to pay their respects in jeans, cuz that's all they got. People understand that. Now let us through."

She tried to sidearm past the host, but he stepped in front of her. Looking the long way up at him, she spat, "People supposed to dress up for planes too, and shows, but no one's got no respect anymore. You don't see them getting' kicked out, do ya?"

"What's going on?" Jesse asked from behind me.

"Nothing," I clipped. Then to Gram and Ethel, "I'll head to the buffet, okay? You have a nice dinner."

"Whoa." Jesse put a hand on my arm. "What's up?"

"He is not dressed appropriately," the host informed, for everyone to hear. I cringed, then winced as Navy came around the corner.

Holy horses was that a dress.

I'd loved that simple jean and t-shirt get-up, but *dude*. Bare back and shoulders, deep V, spaghetti straps, a small triangle cutout at her waist, and slits to her knees so her legs could slip through. Add that to her shy smile and nothing else mattered.

Jesse got caught up too. We were in it together, sucked into a vacuum. Like when you're on a horse and get into stride. Nothing but you and tunnel vision. Nothing but us and Navy.

She looked down to her toes. And those heels. I might have made a squeaking noise.

A younger host hopped up to grab Navy, Delilah, and Guy. Of course he did. Jesse and I watched her rear end, even after it was obstructed by one of the half-walls that separated the space here and there.

Jesse's dad smacked him on the arm, snapping us out of it. "I need some food," he said, fingering over another host to seat them.

"Yeah, you do," Jesse muttered. Then to me, "Come on, I'll get you something to wear." He slid his shiny black shoes against my scuffed cowboy boots. "No problem."

Navy

When Isaiah finally made it to the table—Liza had filled my mom in like they were old gossiping buddies—he looked both amazingly hot and totally gay.

Jesse's clothes were too tight on him, of course, but the right length. The pinstripe button down was glued against his well-defined muscles, and with every reach of his arm, his bicep popped. I grinned.

Jesse squinted his eyes in question. Nodding toward Isaiah, I ran my fingers down my torso. Jesse chuckled and flexed his muscles like a weightlifter.

I nearly snorted into my napkin as Balasz set a plate down in front of Isaiah, who immediately blanched. "I am not eating this."

"Sir?"

"Of course you're eating it," Liza said. "It's ordered and it's not going to waste." Balasz would definitely bring out three more dishes for Isaiah to try if he thought that would make him happy.

Isaiah shook his head. "No."

A lovely array of sliced portabellos was fanned out over the thick linguine, and Balasz's hand darted out to grab the offending plate and take it away.

Liza's fingers clamped down on his wrist. "Are you going to eat this Balasz?"

"No, ma'am."

"Someone else in that kitchen gonna eat it?"

He shook his head.

"Then it ain't goin' nowhere." She glared at Isaiah. "You

know how I feel about waste, Zay. This'll taste just like mine."

"I like yours because you don't put mushrooms in it."

"Well, it still done tastes like mushrooms."

"You use a can, Gram."

Guy motioned Balasz over while running a hand up and down and over and across my mom's bare back so frantically it made me sick. Her tight, black sheath of a dress was cut low and strapless, a straight line all the way around except for the perfect V at the front center, revealing her shallow cleavage. "Can you make the stroganoff without the mushrooms?" he asked.

"I'm fine." Isaiah said it so loud the next table and their waiter turned toward us. "I don't need to eat. I'll grab something at the buffet later."

Jesse stood up, leaned over the table so his long bony arm could reach the dish, then dragged it back to his place setting. "I got this," he announced, before grabbing a fork and quickly shoving all the mushrooms into his mouth as if their very existence was a problem he was going to solve.

I grinned, and Isaiah slumped back in his chair with a twitch of relief on his face.

Jesse held up his fork between bites—"Go ahead and give him my steak, Balasz, thank you."—then went back to shoveling stroganoff into his mouth faster than I could pick up my fork.

He was done before the rest of us and made a show of

stretching his neck out like he'd finished a race. Placing his palms against the edge of the table, he pushed back to straighten his arms, and asked, "So, what'd everyone do today?"

"A little bit of everything and a whole lot of nothing," Guy said. "Which is what I love about vacation."

"I bought a painting," Ethel said. "Won at Bingo, and bought myself a gift."

Liza sighed. "I lost at Bingo."

"I doubled my alcohol consumption," Jesse's dad offered.

Everyone paused for a moment, until Jesse tapped his fingers to the table. "We returned someone's lost purse," he announced.

"You mean, you almost got arrested," Isaiah corrected.

"Really?" Mom worked a scolding frown toward me. "Dare I say trouble?"

I gave her a look. "It wasn't like that." And to steer the conversation back to where it should be, I added, "I spent way too long getting ready, hours that I cannot get back." Getting 'dolled up' took time, as my mom would say. Fact was, all a doll could do was sit and look pretty. Maybe move her limbs this way and that, and turn her head a bit, but she couldn't dance or swim or climb a tree or really even get off the shelf unless someone helped her. What was there to enjoy about that?

"You look amazing though," Jesse said, his voice and gaze reverent.

I felt the blush fill my cheeks and hoped it wasn't obvious with all the make-up my mom had made me put on. *I can tell you didn't use concealer, Navy, go cover up those freckles. Why no blush? Go put on some blush. Did you use powder? The powder is necessary to soften the look and keep your T-zone from getting oily. Okay, good, but one more round of mascara, please.*

All that time wasted, when we could have been playing a game of Rummy 500.

"Not that you look bad the other way," Isaiah added. His grandma cocked her head at him.

"Yeah, no, not what I meant," Jesse said.

"But I second what he said." Isaiah pointed at Jesse.

I smiled and looked to the table. My mom nudged me with her knee, then dug two fingers into my thigh.

She read men thirty times better than I did, and she was confirming I had two choices here. Two options. One kiss.

Smiling at Isaiah, she leaned forward in his direction, a silent message to me that this was who she'd pick. I glanced at Guy, with his pompous face on, and decided that was really a vote in Jesse's favor. "I hear you're going to Harvard next year," she said.

Liza's head came up out of her stroganoff so fast her bob wobbled. "Who you hear that from?" She finished chewing and swallowed. "He's got no plans. That's his problem."

"I could go to Harvard if I wanted," he muttered, loosening

the tie he was wearing and undoing the top button of the borrowed dress shirt.

"Pshaw, you ain't got the grades for Harvard."

Isaiah crossed his arms and forced his lips together. He was so tense, his muscles so clenched, I was afraid he might bust a seam in Jesse's shirt. And that's when I remembered he'd said he had a GED. Did a person have a chance at Harvard with a GED?

"Let's go swimming," Jesse suggested, pushing back in his seat.

"God, yes." Isaiah shot up so fast he had to catch his chair from tumbling over.

I looked between my unfinished salad and Isaiah's discomfort, but it didn't take much to decide. If they were going swimming, I was going swimming. Anyway, I'd already polished off the beets and goat cheese, and those were my favorite parts anyway. As I dropped my napkin over my plate, my mom put a hand to my arm. "Baby, you'll ruin that lovely hair."

"It's okay, Mom, you'll see it again. We have one more formal dinner." Sliding out of my chair, I followed Jesse through the maze of tables, trying to decide how mad I was that Isaiah had fed me lies. And that I'd bought them, that I hadn't put two and two together when he'd stood in front of me in the hall last night.

I hated lies. I hated liars. And I hated that I hadn't even

noticed the contradiction.

Isaiah

Seeing her in a bikini was even better than seeing her in dressage wear. And watching her splash around with that smile on her face was even better than the bikini.

The water rushed from one side of the pool to the other. Couldn't really feel the ship moving, but here was the proof. Up and over the lip, onto the tiles, spilling out across the lounge area. Then it all came back to slosh over the other side.

"It's warmer in the water!" Navy called, as Jesse fought to get her under. They'd been wrestling since we got here. Probably because Alaskan night air was nearly frigid.

"I didn't figure you a swimmer," Bern was spread out on the lounge chair next to mine, hands behind his head.

"You either," I countered. "Didn't figure you'd want to mess up that hair."

He snorted out a short laugh. "Damn straight."

"Bern!" Jesse yelped. "Help!" Then he went under. Navy came up with hands in the air, a victory pose, until Jesse tackled her at her waist.

"Kids." I tsked. "Where do they get their energy?"

"From the sexual tension," Bern replied.

I waved it off. Was he right, though? Was I losing ground?

"Hot tub?" he asked.

"Sure." The hot tub wouldn't get my cowboy hat wet. Of course, three seconds after we slid in, Aunt Ethel walked through, pumping her arm back and forth in a hectic wave. I jumped up, called for Navy and Jesse to join us. And hurry. Please. Before Ethel went and told Gram I was on a romantic spa date.

She was on my side, though, so hopefully . . .

I stood until Ethel was out of sight, then sat back down next to Bern. It would make life a lot easier if people didn't always have to be categorized and filed away in their appropriate slots.

That's what I liked about the ranch. They minded their own business. At least where I worked. We were too busy to be worried about labeling people. Too busy to do anything but take care of shit and get the job done. Everything else fell to the side. Plus, when it was a gay cowboy who hired you, you'd best know to be respectful.

Navy and Jesse crawled out of the pool. I tried not to be obvious about watching her. Jesse tumbled into the hot tub like an unsteady colt, and Navy slid down next to me. Sitting on her other side, Jesse rested both arms along the back edge. A sly way to work an arm around her.

I brushed my fingers against hers. A test disguised as an accident. She yanked away, a flinch.

"Hands are germ factories," she informed.

"Hands dipped in chlorine are probably pretty safe," I

countered, hoping it was that simple and not that he'd already won.

Wrinkling her nose, she glanced at Bern, who was pushing steam up toward his face, then back to me. "What's the deal with you and Harvard?"

Ah, so that's why I'd lost some ground. I studied the sculpted pole to the left of us. "Just because I haven't applied yet doesn't mean I'm not going."

"Isaiah. You can't decide now, in July, that you want to go to Harvard next year and think that's going to happen. Why lie?"

To impress you. Couldn't say it, though. "You haven't lied about anything? To a bunch of people you'll probably never see again and will only know for a week?" I raised my brow. "Come on."

"No, I haven't. I have nothing to hide, and I do not lie." She looked at Bern.

He held his hands out, palms up. "Open book over here."

When it was Jesse's turn, he scratched the tattoo on the back of his elbow.

"Gram wants me to do something big," I lied. She wanted me to do something normal and small, actually. Something steady and boring. "I'm trying to figure out what that would be. Maybe I can't do the ranch forever, but it's all I have. It's all I know." I searched her eyes for the sympathy I'd seen there last night. I didn't want to lay it all out again in front of these guys. *Please understand. Don't hold it against me. You get what it's like, right? Wanting to find a place where you can still feel your dad?*

I imagined the ship rocking her calm, back and forth. Water flowed up and over her chest, flipped off her shoulders onto the blue and white tile, then back again. I imagined my thoughts were part of that calm, coaxing her back to the connection we'd had last night. She'd pushed for it. She'd pushed me to open up.

We stared at each other. She linked her pinky across mine. A split second, then it was gone, as was her attention.

But it was something.

Navy

Turning to Jesse, I resisted the urge to trace the dark piano keys on his pale skin. It looked like there was no scarring, no raised lines, no scratch, nothing. I wanted to feel it, to make sure, but touching someone usually took me weeks, if not months.

"Amazing how it looks so much like a sketch on a piece of paper," I said instead.

"Thanks." He pulled his arm down from where it was propped up so I could get a better look. "My grandpa's a pro. You can tell the few he didn't do on my dad, just from looking at them."

"The earring and the moon?" I guessed. They looked rough,

like they were old and from a dingy basement somewhere.

Jesse nodded into a proud grin. "He did those himself, when he was learning," he explained.

I coughed in disbelief. The small slice of moon was *on his face.*

"My mom did one on his thigh, which obviously you can't see, but it's smooth too, just more feminine."

"Your mom tattoos?" Hadn't he said she worked for the cruise line?

"Right, no, well, she used to." He looked down at his arm.

"Can I feel?" I asked. We had been wrestling in the pool, after all.

I was comfortable with him already, I realized. The contradiction of him set me at ease, a guy who walked around dressed in rebel art, yet was petrified of doing the wrong thing or getting into trouble. A guy who'd jumped in to calm me down when Isaiah looked at me like I stole a purse, then resolved to put himself in the line of fire to return it. For a girl he hardly knew. We'd been on the same page about everything today, even if we were essentially strangers.

Only he didn't make me feel like a stranger. He didn't make me feel alone. And he was nodding.

Clearing my throat, I traced the piano keys in their progression from harsh and clear to scratchy and abstract, to something that was almost a heartbeat.

"Is this a heartbeat?" I was easily aware of my own, with the hum of the bubbles and the sway of the boat, our faces so close together I couldn't tell if the heat was from him or from the hot tub steam rising between us.

"Sound waves." His voice a gentle, charged, lulling rumble.

I smiled into it. "Even better."

"Bears taste best in the fall," Isaiah said.

My hand trailed down Jesse's arm, disappearing into the water, and we all turned to him.

"All right, Cowboy." Bern slapped at the water with his palm. "Tell us about the bears."

"Oh, forget it," he muttered.

"No way." I laughed. "You can't say bears taste better in the fall and leave it at that. First, what does a bear taste like? And why are they better in the fall?"

"It's a gamey meat. Fatty though. They're better because they've been eating fish and berries. Not coming off hibernation like in the spring."

"ATTENTION PASSENGERS: THIS IS A REMINDER THAT THERE IS A LOST AND FOUND AT THE PASSENGER SERVICES DESK ON DECK SIX. IF YOU HAVE FOUND ANYTHING TODAY THAT WASN'T YOURS, PLEASE PROCEED TO THAT LOST AND FOUND. ALSO, IF YOU WERE IN THE CASINO OR THE PIANO BAR TODAY, WE WOULD LIKE TO SPEAK WITH YOU. PLEASE HEAD TO PASSENGER SERVICES PROMPTLY AND OTHERWISE SAFEGUARD ALL YOUR VALUABLES."

"Does that mean me?" Jesse asked.

"Doesn't mean me," Isaiah said. "I was only there for a second."

"*We* were only there for a second," I corrected. "And we have to. If we don't, and they have cameras, it's even more suspicious."

"Wait. You all were in the piano bar?" Bern asked.

"I need to find Toni," Jesse said, hopping up and out. He ran dripping for the towels and rushed back to us. We stared at him.

"Toni?" I asked. "Really?"

Shaking the towel at me, he explained, "I need more info first, anything that would separate me, make me seem less guilty. Otherwise, my nerves . . ."

Yeah, we'd seen his nerves. No one could argue with that.

Jesse

I wiped my sweaty palms on the towel around my waist, but it wasn't very dry either. We were sopping wet and barely clothed, so I was trying to catch Toni's eye from the doorway, only she was busy with her hands deep inside someone's hair.

"Is she trying to make them all look like her?" Navy whispered at my shoulder. I turned my head and our noses nearly touched. I mean, I had a sizeable nose, but that still seemed pretty close for her comfort. Closer even than in the hot tub.

She didn't jump away though. Her eyeliner was smudged from the pool, and her hair squeezed out and twisted over her shoulder. She was wearing my shirt because she'd dropped hers on the floor by her flip-flops and it was soaked.

Isaiah was leaning against the gold banister of the stairs, hands in his pockets, eyes on her ass. My shirt fell just below her butt when she was standing up, but leaning over?

I shook my head but couldn't really blame him. Even now, when my head was on the chopping block and perspiration streaming from my armpits, she was distracting me too.

She looked back toward Toni, who was indeed braiding little bits of a girl's hair exactly like her own. Another coordinator was doing the same right next to her, and the third was alone with a curling iron.

Navy nudged me with her elbow and nodded to a group on the couch. They all had the Toni braids too, some pulled back into ponytails, some loose and long. "This is hardly a true makeover party," Navy muttered. "They clearly have never met Delilah Carmichael."

Walking swiftly in, I tapped Toni on the shoulder, then turned to make my way right back out.

She handed off an unfinished braid to the girl whose hair she was doing, then followed, bursting through the doorway with her smile. "Hey guys! What's going on? Heard you ran into Benoît! He's great, right?"

"Yeah." I shifted from foot to foot. "About that, you know

anything more about this new announcement?"

"Only that casino chips are missing, but it happened in the piano bar."

"Do you know when? Like, what time it was?"

She knocked her shoulder into mine. "You can't be playing PI and messing up the investigation, Jesse."

"Please, do you know what time?"

She frowned, a wide spread almost as severe as her smile. "I don't actually. And I think you should drop it. After today, it's only going to make you look guilty."

"Yeah, well, that's the problem. I was in the piano bar for a little bit this afternoon—"

"*We* were in the piano bar a little bit this afternoon," Navy corrected.

"And your security buddy already doesn't seem to like me very much," I continued. "So I'm trying to figure out what to do here. I'm supposed to go in, right? But I'm innocent."

"So let Navy lead. He liked her." And with this, she poked Navy in the side.

Navy frowned and wrapped her arms around herself, while I shot out a, "He is clearly too old for her."

"Please, he's not that much older than me." And Toni swung her body side to side, back and forth.

"Listen, I came to you first because it would make me feel better going in if I knew we weren't there at the same time as the thief."

She stopped rocking and studied me, her lips a clean line. "When were you there?"

I glanced back at Isaiah and Navy, and Navy pulled out her phone. "My mom texted me at two seventeen."

"That's right. You were with us before that, remember? I woke up, went straight to the buffet, ate lunch with these guys, sat around for awhile, you came by, then the purse happened, and then my dad. Maybe we were with Benoît when the crap went down in the piano bar?" I took Toni's hand. "Please, *please* tell me I don't have anything to be worried about."

She smiled. "I'll vouch for you, Jesse, of course. And with that timeline, you should be safe."

"You promise?"

She nodded.

Thank God. I threw my arms around her in relief.

"But you should still go in," she added, voice strained because I must have been squeezing too tight. "So you don't look guilty, okay?"

Letting go of her, I nodded. "Right."

Navy tugged at the towel hanging around my shoulders. "Can we change first?" she asked.

That's when Isaiah said, "Hey, doesn't your mom work for the cruise line? Can't you just call her?"

Navy

Benoît stood in front of Jesse's stateroom as we turned the corner. Isaiah kept walking, but Jesse stopped so quick I ran into him, tumbling us both forward a few feet.

My hand was already on his arm because of the near fall, and his face was draining of color, so I slid my palm against his and held my breath. Like in the hot tub, it didn't feel so bad. The fact that he needed comfort overrode everything else. I exhaled slowly as he clasped on, then held still in the beats that followed. I could do this. I could hold someone's hand like a normal girl, and I wasn't even searching for the nearest hand sanitizer station. Thinking about it maybe, but not looking for it. With a grin, I squeezed once. As if jumpstarted, Jesse nodded and moved toward his room.

"Looking for Jesse?" Isaiah asked Benoît.

The security officer looked up, then down at his notes, at the room number, and back to us. "*Non*. A Vincent Kowalski."

"That's my dad," Jesse said, his hand gripping tighter to mine.

Benoît raised a thick unibrow. "Your dad was in the bar today."

"He's as honest as they come."

Looking down at his papers, Benoît flipped the top one around. It was the boarding photo of the two of them. "I should have recognized you," he said, tapping at the picture with his pen. Wally's arms were crossed and the tattoos wound up both arms, an array of images: feathers, cherries, a raining umbrella, lightning, roses, and a thick forearm cuff of waves. What made him look sinister, though, was the ink crawling up his neck, plus the circle tattooed around an empty earring hole, and the small moon at his temple.

"We were there too," I said, figuring it better to get that out of the way before it seemed like we were hiding something. "We were changing and then coming to find you, because of the announcement."

I could feel the damp coolness of Jesse's swim trunks near the back of my hand, and he smelled like chlorine, more than the rest of us. Isaiah and I had changed first, while Jesse paced the hallway.

Benoît nodded at the door next to him. "You going to let me in?"

Jesse let go of my hand to open the door, then held it against the wall for us as we all filed through. His room was colored the same as mine—tan and white with oak and a little floral wallpaper—but only had one bathroom, one closet/hall, and one bedroom area with the same desk, lamp, TV, and huge mirror hanging on the wall. The little living room was half the size of ours, with a couch, table, and a chair. At the other end, the patio doors led out to a shrunken balcony just big enough for two chairs and a tiny side table.

"I only came to ask if he saw something." Benoît scanned the long, thin room. "His bar receipts clock him as being there for quite some time." With this he raised the unibrow again in Jesse's direction. "Not so straight to spend all day in a bar, I wouldn't say." He moved to the desk and pulled open the drawer, his fingers rifling through. "But now as I promised you earlier, since I'm already here, I think it might be time to search your room. Would you like to have a seat?"

We didn't move.

"Not a question or a suggestion," Benoît said, turning to face us. "All of you, sit." Then he radioed to have someone named Bruiser join him.

Jesse and I shared a look before following Isaiah to the couch, while Benoît began to take apart the closet.

"Tell him your mom works for the cruise line," Isaiah hissed, not loud enough that the officer would hear it.

"No." Jesse's fingers were methodically rubbing his elbow. "I'm not dragging her into this. We're innocent, and they'll figure that out, and I don't want a mark on her record."

"It's not a mark. Maybe she can help."

"It's not your room being searched, you don't get to decide."

The door banged open, and Bruiser loomed large enough that we snapped our mouths shut.

Jesse

Bruiser was three times the size of Benoît and spoke mostly in grunts. Somehow Benoît understood him, and they tore apart the room in seventeen minutes. Every drawer, the empty suitcases under our beds, the open safe we hadn't bothered putting anything in, under the couch, in the couch cushions, between the sheets, inside the pillow cases, and even the ceiling cubby above the couch where the pull-down bunk was stored.

Places I hadn't known existed, even if I'd been trying to hide something.

"What time were you in the bar?" Benoît asked once they'd finished. He and Bruiser now stood in front of where we were lined up on the couch.

"Maybe two-thirty?" I guessed. My swimsuit had me feeling damp all over, like I was leaking guilt that wasn't even mine.

"Who do you remember seeing?"

"My dad," I mumbled. Then, louder, "The bartender."

"The piano guy," Navy offered. "Who really could use a lesson or two."

"You play piano?" Isaiah asked.

"A little. One of my mom's boyfriends taught me."

I wiped my palms back and forth on my swim trunks, a little calmer now that they hadn't found anything in the room. Of course, I'd known they wouldn't find what had been stolen, but for some reason I was thinking there'd be a poster board somewhere announcing how my mom had left us and did not in fact work for the cruise line. Having your stuff torn apart felt like all your secrets were being unearthed.

"Okay." Benoît slapped his notebook closed. "Cleared again." He pointed his pen at me. "So no pit for you, yet. Now where's your father?"

"Isn't he cleared too?" I asked. "If he was guilty, you'd have found something."

"Anyway, shouldn't you be looking for someone who was also near the first victim in line?" Isaiah asked. "Someone who was in both places?"

Benoît raised an eyebrow. "That sir, would be you."

Isaiah held the officer's gaze like he had nothing to prove. Man, I wished I had steel balls like his.

"How do you know that?" Navy asked, glancing between them.

"The photos," Benoît replied. "The camera roll is in order of how you boarded the ship."

Isaiah opened his mouth, closed it, then laughed. "That's kind of brilliant. So the whole point isn't even to sell a souvenir, but to have a picture of everyone on board?"

"Unless someone skipped the line," I pointed out. "A thief would skip the line."

Benoît's gaze slid to me. "Perhaps you shouldn't suggest that, because you were NOT a suspect based on proximity to the original victim. Unless you skipped."

I tried to stay calm and cool like Isaiah had, but three seconds and I was looking away, biting my lip, willing Benoît to stop and focus on someone—something—else.

"Call your dad and ask where we can meet him."

Hanging my head, I agonized over my reply. "I can't."

"Why not?"

"Because I'm not allowed to use my phone."

"Shady," Bruiser grunted.

"It's expensive," I mumbled. And I'd already used it three times more than I should've today, not that my mom had replied even once. I guess maybe if I used it again, Dad would think *this* was why there were charges. Would it itemize them? I pulled my phone out. "Okay. Okay."

Security wants to know where you are. Did you hear the announcement?

He replied immediately: *Send them over. And stop using your phone.*

Where are you? I asked.

Where do you think?

I sighed and looked up. "Pretty sure he's back in the piano bar."

Isaiah

"How are you so calm like that?" Jesse asked, as the door swung shut on Benoît and Bruiser.

I leaned back to stretch my arm along the back of the couch. "So calm like what?"

Navy snorted. "Like a statue. Are you used to being in

trouble?"

"Shit hits the fan, and I get more chill, I guess. That's not a personality flaw." They shared a look. Like I was shady and they were clean. But I hadn't had to be shady since my dad died. "What? It's over. We can put it behind us now and pretend we're on vacation."

"We are on vacation," Navy muttered.

"Sure doesn't feel like it," Jesse countered.

Navy nodded. "My nerves are shot."

"What time is it?" Jesse checked his phone. "Nine? Why does it feel like midnight?"

"Because it's midnight in Omaha," I pointed out.

"And because of the stress," Navy added, sliding down further into the couch, letting her cheek fall against the cushion, closing her eyes. "Let's go to bed and then tomorrow we can pretend none of this happened."

"Or we could sneak into Bingo," Jesse said. "I think we can play if we're with an adult. Think Dee or Liza are there right now?"

"You don't strike me as the Bingo type," Navy murmured, half asleep.

"Well, no way I can sleep after that, and since I know how you two feel about the teen lounge . . ."

She smirked without opening an eye.

"The two of us are cooked," I noted.

"Really?" But Jesse was looking at her, not me. "You're

gonna leave me hanging?"

"Isn't that what Bern's for?" Navy asked. "And the teen lounge?"

"And Toni," I added. "Making out with eager older girls. Isn't that what vacation is all about?"

Navy opened her eyes on me. Jesse furrowed his brow. "I've never really been into that kind of thing. Anyway, she's way too old to go for me."

I laughed while Navy sputtered out a disbelieving cough.

"She isn't?" he asked, looking back and forth between us.

"She has thrown herself at you every chance she's had." Navy sat up. "Please, Jesse, be the upstanding young man I think you are and stay away from her."

"Or do what every reasonable male would do and hit that."

Navy sneered at me. The way I figured it, though, Jesse was the only thing standing between me and my ranch.

Day 3: Ketchikan
6:30 a.m. – 3:00 p.m.

Navy

As we stepped off the boat, my phone beeped: *You up?*

It was Isaiah, of course. According to my mom, Jesse and Bern had crashed Bingo last night as she was leaving. She'd left them her cards and daubers. Who knows how long they'd stayed up.

Just made it on land. You?

In line to come out.

"Hey Mom? I'm gonna wait for Isaiah, okay?"

"Of course you are, dear." She waggled her eyebrows. I did my best to ignore it. No twitch, no frown, no reaction whatsoever.

"Make sure you call if he doesn't show." Guy adjusted his dark linen scarf inside the upturned collar of his trench. "I don't want you wandering Alaska alone."

I held my cell up. "He *just* texted me."

"Please, Guy. No one leaves a Carmichael lady in the lurch." My mom linked an arm through his, then spanned out in front of her with the other. "And this Alaska is very small town. I wouldn't worry about her."

As she led him forward, he looked over his shoulder and threw his fingers up against his ear like they were a phone. I wasn't worried about finding them if I needed to—my mom was in tomato red pants and matching heels. With the cement port for the cruise ships about as massive as the town itself, she'd be easy to spot.

Waving them off, I tried to load my *Language Learner!* app on a stilted middle-of-nowhere connection. Really, I should be glad the texts were coming through.

Isaiah's boots tipped me off to his approach, and he greeted me with a lazy cowboy *Mornin'*.

I tucked my cell away and smiled.

As we walked toward town, I took pictures with my phone. What we could see of Ketchikan was built on a hillside. Quaint and no-frills, the houses were nearly stacked on top of each other as they climbed the grade. The sidewalk and road along the water led into a dark concrete tunnel, and cars rumbled by as we made our way through.

We emerged to a picture-perfect postcard, with snow-topped mountains looming close behind the squat downtown area. The buildings had a colonial feel to them, and the signs all directed us to historic Creek Street, the original settlement propped up on wooden decking along a wide creek. We wandered through the old clapboard cabins that were once trading posts, pointing things out to each other as we went:

"Alaska's first city."

"Salmon capital of the world."

"There's really no shortage of moccasins."

"*Hell-o, Dolly, well hell-o Dolly, it's so nice to have you back where you belong.*"

"Wait. The whore?" Isaiah planted his feet outside the actual, real life Dolly's house, as if a cowboy had never entered a brothel.

The woman in the doorway of the now museum stiffened. "She was never a whore. She was a *sporting* woman. Conversation and drinks only. Perhaps you should come in and educate yourself."

"She made money off of conversation and drinks?" He repeated, still frozen.

"Like a personal bartender?" I asked.

She puffed her chest out as if she were Dolly Arthur herself. "Exactly."

Isaiah took a few steps back to lean against the deck railing. "I'll wait for you here."

I slid closer to him with a grin. "Prefer sporting *men*, do you?"

He crossed his arms with a frown.

"Sorry, that was uncalled for." I skipped away from Dolly's for his sake. "Your gram told my mom is all. I didn't believe it."

His boots clapped on the decking behind me for a few paces. Then, quieter than normal, he said, "I'd kiss you right now, to be honest."

Turning around and walking backward in front of him, I considered stopping and letting him do just that. He'd kiss me, and I'd be done with it, the first time, but Jesse's face popped in my mind. His was the hand I felt more inclined to hold. He was the one I hoped wouldn't think too much of Isaiah and me spending the morning together. Falling into step next to him, I let the moment pass. "Is that your vacation goal? Some hot older girl like you told Jesse?"

"Except you're not older," he pointed out.

Stopping abruptly, I turned to him. "I don't make a habit of kissing boys who lie to me."

He opened his mouth and took a breath like he was going to say something, then closed it. It was a beautiful mouth, but becoming less and less enticing as the minutes ticked by, as the lies added up. "I didn't mean to make anything awkward." He set a hand on the rail and ran it along the wood, asking for a splinter and likely also an infection. "But for the record, I'd kiss you even if I didn't have anything to prove."

"Kissing someone doesn't prove anything." And if I was simply something for him to prove, then again, no thank you.

"It would convince Gram," he muttered.

"So what if your grandma thinks you're gay?"

"It's about a bet."

"That's silly." Ignorant too, but I didn't think he'd appreciate me insulting his grandma.

"Yeah, well, there's more to it than that, but the point is she won't let me go back to the ranch because of it, which wouldn't be a problem if it wasn't all I wanted in the whole world." He took a deep breath and shook his head. "I'm sorry I lied to you about Harvard. I thought if I could impress you, if she saw me with you this week, maybe she'd drop it, you know?"

"So you lied to me, manipulated me, and used me to get what you wanted."

Hanging his head, he sighed. "I'm truly sorry, that's all I have. It won't happen again."

I tapped my foot until he looked back up. Even with a convincing display of regret, he was still the steel statue—no trembling, no cracks. "Why's the ranch so important?"

"I told you, I can feel my dad there. I love the horses and the work and the wilderness and the hunting. Every bit of it, even the dirty days in the rain. It's a way of life my dad tried to choose, but he couldn't let go of everything else and that made him miserable. I'm all in. I want to be all in. I vowed, at his funeral, to be all in. I *will* let go of everything else, if that's what it takes."

I studied him for a minute. The length of him and the relaxed pose, the muscles lining his forearms from the clenched fists—fists which were about the only emotion he was letting show, aside from the tone of his voice, desperate toward the end of his speech. Though why he needed me when he just admitted he'd let go of everything to have the ranch, I didn't know.

Nodding, I turned toward the creek. It wasn't a rushing stream here, but a placid pool of murky water. The tall poles and wooden beams of the decking formed a nearly complete circle around it.

Isaiah rested his elbows on the railing and pointed out two seals.

We watched them in silence for awhile, and I took more pictures—of the seals, the historic brick and almost pink and sky blue buildings across the way, Isaiah's profile and his hat, and my shoes next to his boots. I even got a selfie of the two of us, which I was pretty happy with since his dimples showed up, as long as you knew where to look for them.

The truth of him was like that too, like his dimples. You could find it if you knew where to look. And maybe it didn't show up all the time, but when it did, you couldn't look away in case you missed it, because peeking into those cracks and fissures left you wanting more.

Isaiah

It felt like a first date, three hours in Ketchikan alone. Like vacation too, like we were a regular couple. We had lunch in a small deli next to the water. At one point, Navy laughed so hard her head fell over the table, hair drifting across my fingers. Granted, my arm was stretched out in case she wanted to hold my hand. But still, her hair.

Then her phone started blowing up.

"Bern wants to know where we are," she explained, fingers working to tell him. "We're going to meet him by the totem." She laughed. "He says 'Hey, did you see this totem? It's the real deal.'"

We got there in five minutes. Bern's neck was craned so far back he looked inhuman.

Navy snickered. "If you stand back, you can see it better."

"If I stand back, it loses its wonder," he replied.

She shoved at him and he stumbled. "Where's Jesse?" she asked.

"Should we SOS him?"

"Definitely. I think this is an emergency, don't you?"

"That the three of us are together, and he's not here?" I asked.

"Exactly." She beamed at me, then went back to her phone.

"It's okay, Cowboy," Bern said, lifting his face back to the sky. "Look at the totem. Feel the totem. Center that jealousy."

I shushed him, but Navy was oblivious as she waited for a response. Did she wait for me like that, when she was with Jesse and I wasn't around? How could I make my intentions clear, that she wasn't only a vacation conquest or something to prove?

Hi, I'm serious about you, your vibe, and holy horse crap that hair. Yeah, no.

"How long do we wait?" Bern asked.

"Should I text him again?"

"No, he's not going to text you back, remember? If he got it, he'll find us."

"Oh, right. Good point." She tapped the screen, as if willing him to jump through it.

"Ten minutes," I said.

Her head jerked up. "If he's still on the boat, that won't be enough time."

"Well, we aren't gonna sit around for him all day, are we?"

Navy's face fell, and I wanted to take it back.

"Half hour, then?"

She looked up at the wooden eagle topping the pole. "Fine."

The totem, beneath the eagle, was a mess of hands, faces, wings, a Pinocchio nose, and too many eyes. All of it was worn and dark, in fading black, red, and blue paint.

Scanning the informational podium, Bern jerked his hand back against his shirt. "Ew! The paint is made with salmon eggs."

"You're afraid of salmon eggs?" I asked, as Navy scanned the street.

"Not like they'd be gooey or fertile anymore," Navy pointed out, glancing back at him.

"Stick your tongue on it then, I dare you," Bern countered.

She wrinkled her nose. "There's pretty much nothing I'd stick my tongue on."

"Plus, if salmon are anything like trout, it's only the sac they come in that's gooey."

They both stared at me.

"What?"

"You've been up close and personal with trout eggs?" Bern asked.

With a short laugh, Navy replied, "Of course he has."

I shrugged. "Wilderness caviar."

"He catches them, then rips the fish apart with his bare hands." Bern curled his back. Stretched crooked fingers out in Navy's direction. "Skin first, he peels it back and off, then picks out the bones with his teeth." Straightening from his scary campfire story pose, he looked to me. "Hey, you got a knife on you Cowboy?"

"Well, not here. They wouldn't let me bring it on the boat."

Back in position, he continued, "Then he takes out his machete and slices up that mommy fish until he can find her babies." Bern circled Navy, making her laugh even harder. "Then he rips out the fish uterus and throws mommy, in *slices*,

91

onto the fire to burn. He sits . . . and watches her scream . . . while squeezing baby by baby out of the sac and into his mouth."

"That would never happen," I muttered. "They need a little salt first."

Bern moved out of the way in time for Jesse to come up behind Navy and grab her waist.

She let out a little scream and turned with a laugh, swatting at Bern. "Don't *do* that!"

They both snickered, and Jesse adjusted his cowboy hat.

Wait. What?

"Where did that come from?" I asked.

"First store I walked into. Figured maybe it's indigenous. Do as the Romans, you know?"

I tried not to sneer at the mash-up of a cowboy hat riding atop a hoodie, shorts, and flip flops. "That's *disposable*," I informed him. "Nothing but a souvenir."

Navy threw up one shoulder. "I think it's cute."

Bern studied it, then studied mine. "What's yours made out of, if that one's disposable?"

Trying not to sound haughty, I replied, "Beaver."

The three of them cracked up.

"What?"

"Beaver," Bern snickered. "Lady beaver? Figures cowboys would make their hats out of something like that." This sent Jesse and him over the edge. Navy tried her best to look offended.

"That's gonna lose its shape by the time this trip is over, is all I'm saying."

"Really?" Bern went serious. "Beaver?"

"Yes!" I snapped, pointing to it. "Four hundred bucks for this baby. She's gonna last me a damn long time."

Jesse and Bern lost it again at *this baby*. I threw up my hands and walked away. I wasn't going to waste my time trying to keep Navy's attention off Jesse all day. We'd had our morning alone. Now I needed to do something big. Something she wouldn't forget. Something any girl would understand.

Jesse

We didn't talk about why Isaiah disappeared on us, but I had a hard time keeping the hat on. Not that taking it off and tossing it was any less dorky.

It worked so well for him. When I'd seen them, I thought maybe I could look that cool too. I mean, what did a skinny kid in flip flops, shorts, and t-shirts have on lean muscle in boots, jeans, and a badass hat?

I hated jeans, and I hated socks. But I could do the hat.

It was awfully itchy, though.

I pulled it off to scratch my head and set it in my lap.

We were on a bench near the re-boarding ramp. Bern and Navy were doing that kid's MASH game—mansion, apartment, shack, house—while I worried over the hat. My future had been 'mashed' out on its receipt, Navy's on her souvenir coffee mug receipt, and Bern's on his cured salmon receipt. He'd bought a package for every one of his cousins, and apparently there were a lot of them.

Now they were doing Isaiah, on Bern's thigh. Good thing we had a pen and not a pencil. He'd pulled his plaid shorts up as high as they went, so there was enough room.

"Hey!" Navy called.

Following her gaze, I found the rest of our dinner table working their way past us toward the boat. Well, all but my dad. I wondered if I should text him to make sure he made it back on time. At least he'd pretended to shop with me for fifteen minutes before I'd left him for the totem pole and cowboy hat ridicule. Would he lose track of where he was and what was happening, ending up forgotten at some bar in Ketchikan? How many drinks would that take?

"We're doing MASH for you, Isaiah," Navy said.

"You and Toni are getting married!" Bern sang.

"Tony?" His grandma stopped dead in her tracks, causing everyone to pause behind her.

"Toni is a counselor in the teen lounge," Navy said. "But more importantly, or accurately perhaps, you end up in a shack, on a ranch, with a pet pig." Bern squealed like one, and she waited for him to finish before continuing. "Seven sons, you'll drive a Mercedes, and blah blah blah. Wanna see?" She pointed to Bern's bare thigh.

"No." Isaiah's jaw clenched down on the end of the syllable.

Liza marched the few steps to Isaiah. "Is there something you need to tell me?"

"Toni is a girl," he said, without a glance at her.

"Sure she is."

Navy stood up and rushed forward, her gaze hopping from Isaiah to Liza as if she knew something I didn't. "Liza, she totally is. Toni with an i."

Navy's mom put a hand on Liza's arm. "Don't worry, hon. My daughter will kiss him straight for ya." She turned to Navy with a smile. "Won't you, Baby? First time's a charm."

"Mom!"

"Nice of you to offer, Dee, but it don't work that way."

Isaiah checked his grandma's frown, then booked it for the ship with wide strides, leaving the rest of us behind.

Navy stormed away too, but in a slightly different direction, so Bern and I hustled after her. Tugging at Navy's white tee, he got her to slow down a bit. "What was that about?"

"Nothing."

"Midnight, come on, we're all friends here."

"She was making fun of me."

"Who was making fun of you?"

"My mom!"

"Why would your mom make fun of you?" he asked.

"Why would anyone make fun of you?" I echoed.

She glanced at me for a split second before setting her attention on Bern, like she didn't want me to hear about it. He nodded, and they shuffled forward.

"Guys! Not cool." They stopped, but Navy looked at her feet. Her mom, Guy, Ethel, and Liza passed us, and I waited for them to be out of earshot. "I was the idiot who bought the cowboy hat today, remember?" I held out my hand to show them the proof. "Must I detail why that was so pathetic, or can you all make the connection yourself? Not to mention the snide humiliation I endured under the totem pole?"

Bern turned to Navy in question, but she was still focused on the ground, the toe of her boot—the only change in her outfit aside from the long, delicate chains hanging from her ears—digging itself against the pavement.

"I've never been kissed." She swallowed so heavy I could hear it. "I'm sixteen and have never been kissed."

"You're only sixteen?" I asked.

Her head snapped up to me, a scowl on her face. "Almost seventeen, but that sounds even worse. Thanks for pushing it."

My mouth dropped open to apologize, to tell her how not a big deal that was, but Bern was throwing his arms around her and planting kisses all over her face. Wincing beneath a few scattered bits of laughter, she slid away from him.

"Maybe she wasn't making fun of you," I said, as she wiped her face with her palms and pulled out her hand sanitizer. "Maybe she believes it." I was starting to think she could pretty much turn me anything.

"Oh, please, child," Bern shoved at me, but I didn't take my eyes off her.

"I'll be your first kiss," I offered.

She rubbed her hands together, zipped her purse back up, and sighed at me. "Thanks, Jesse. But I want it to be natural, real, romantic, you know? Not a business deal. Not out of pity."

"For real, Navy, how can you think it would be pity?"

Bern started fanning himself, but we ignored him. It almost felt like a moment right then—hung on a high note, like speaker feedback amping up while the world faded out. All I'd have to do was lean down, tilt her chin up, and press my lips to hers.

I studied the fresh layer of gloss she'd applied during MASH and thought about it, but now that I knew it'd be her first, I felt like I needed to make it amazing. Special. Fireworks on fireworks.

Not to mention, she'd just likened our conversation to a business deal, so she'd probably push me away. And it was Isaiah that she and her mom were talking about. Had they been talking about him and kisses already? Would she even want one from me?

No. Probably not.

Navy took the cowboy hat out of my hand. Placing it on her head, she spun on her heel and headed toward the line forming to board the ship. Her mom, Guy, Ethel, and Liza were way up ahead, and I could no longer see Isaiah.

With the hat on her, they almost made the perfect pair. Then again, it was my hat that she'd wanted, something of mine she'd taken.

If only I'd said I bought it for her in the first place.

Navy

My mom leaned toward the dinner table and put a hand up to the side of her mouth—my side, as if I wouldn't hear. "Did you all see Wally on Creek Street today?" Dropping her hand, she sat back and shook her head. "That kind of drinking cannot be good for a person's soul."

"Is it a regular thing?" Ethel asked Isaiah and me. We looked at each other, but how were we to know?

"I'm not sure I want you hanging out with him," Guy said.

"I'm not hanging out with him. I'm hanging out with his son." *Not to mention, Buddy, I'm sixteen, and you just showed up eight months ago.*

My mom put a hand on my arm. "He's right though, Baby. Maybe you and Isaiah should pair off."

Isaiah's cheek twitched, like he was trying to contain a grin. But at least he came to Jesse's defense: "He's a good kid. And none of us has any way of knowing what's going on with his dad."

"You could ask him," Liza said.

My mom nodded avidly. "Ooh, yes. Ask him."

"Even if I asked him, I wouldn't report back."

Like a flip of a switch, my mom went all smiles and threw up her pageant wave. "Hi, dears! We were just talking about you."

I rolled my eyes as Jesse sat down on Isaiah's other side.

"Have a nice time in Ketchikan today, Wally?" Guy asked.

"Sure," Jesse's dad replied.

"That bar, what was it called? You like the ambience? Maybe the waitress? Or was it the al-key-hall?"

I glared at Guy. What an idiot.

"What I do is really not any of your business," Mr. Kowalski muttered, thankfully without a slur. So at least there was that—less ammunition.

"I wonder if something's missing again today," my mom said, spreading a napkin on her lap.

"Mom! There are a million people on this boat!" I knew an insinuation when I heard one, and I also knew what Dad would think if he could hear her now. I may have been a baby when he died, but she raised me with *Your daddy always said this*, and *Your daddy always said that*, and number one was, and always will be, *Your daddy says we love, we don't hate*.

Only God could know what Mr. Kowalski was going through, and far be it from us, with our limited knowledge and comparatively baby brains, to judge. That's what my dad would've said.

"Nearly 5,000 to be exact," Jesse piped up. "About 3,500 passengers and 1,500 crew."

"How do you know that?" his dad asked.

"Danilo," Jesse replied. "Our room attendant."

Wally snorted while Mom rolled her eyes to me and said, "Maybe it's all a ruse, his wife working on a cruise ship. Maybe this is what they *do*."

Wally raised an eyebrow at Jesse, who sunk in his seat, jaw twitching.

"Defend yourself!" I cried, throwing an arm out. Mainly I was talking to Jesse, because I wouldn't speak to an adult like that, but sure, his dad too. Why were they just taking it?

"What's there to defend?" Mr. Kowalski asked, resting a forearm out on the table and fiddling with his silverware. "I drank my day away, and I plan to drink my night away. If I'm lucky, I'll drink this whole vacation away, and then maybe I'll be okay with what I'm going home to."

Well, that shut us up.

For a moment anyway.

"It must be hard having your wife away for six months at a time." Ethel clucked. "A mother really shouldn't do that."

Mr. Kowalski looked to Jesse again, and again Jesse avoided eye contact.

"His drinking doesn't make him a thief," Jesse muttered. "I mean, drinking makes him clumsy, not sneaky. There's nothing shady about a drunk."

"There's a lot shady about a drunk," Liza said.

"Bless your heart," my mom added, reaching as far as she could across me, her arm stretching over my plate as she tried to lay a hand on him.

"He doesn't need you to bless his heart," I snapped, wanting to beat her with all she'd taught me until it wiped her gossip clean and made her happy again.

Balasz ambled over with his fancy leather pad and pen at the ready. "Have we decided what we shall be eating this night?"

Wally stood. "I've decided I won't be."

We watched him go, then Liza stuck a finger in the air and ordered, as if nothing had gone down. Didn't they realize we had to share meals with him the rest of the trip? Was I sitting with a bunch of children?

"I can't believe you guys," I muttered, interrupting Guy between "Caesar" and "salad."

Ethel stared at me, steely-eyed. "Good riddance."

And without a word or a glance, Jesse bolted almost as fast as his father.

Isaiah

"Can we not go to the teen lounge?" I asked Navy as we left the dinner hall. I knew she was itching to get away from the adults but was hoping she wouldn't be antsy to find Jesse quite yet.

I had big plans for the night.

"I hate it as much as you, but what if Jesse's waiting for us?"

"It's more likely Bern is waiting for us," I pointed out. "It didn't seem like Jesse wanted company."

"So weird, right, that he wouldn't look at us?"

"Maybe he knows something."

Navy stopped in front of the elevator and faced me. Hands on her hips. "Not you, too."

I put a palm in the air. "Not me, too." Fighting with her didn't work into my plans.

The doors slid open. We stepped inside. Navy didn't move to press a button, so I hit the one I wanted. The one that would get us to the floor where you could walk outside around the entire ship. Once off the elevator, the wooden and windowed double doors were easy to find. Difficult to open though, and heavy due to the wind, which was harsh as a whip.

Clutching my hat to keep it on my head, I offered her my other hand. She studied it. "Did you wash your hands after dinner?"

"No. Did you?"

Shaking her head, she denied me, but with a pained look on her face. Okay, but it wasn't about me. It was about the germs. I led her to the back end of the ship.

The sunset had drawn a few other couples, but it wasn't packed. It should've been. A blazing and brilliant orange had swallowed everything in sight: the water, the mountains, even the clouds.

Navy's waist braced the rail, her mouth open a whisper. Delicate chains dangled from her ears and swirled in the wind. An orange tinge shaded her face and hair, which I did not reach out to touch. Not yet.

I smiled. "Just in time."

"It's ..."

"It is," I agreed.

From blazing, the sunset fell to soft peaches. Little by little, it receded, giving the sea and sky back their blue. The blue was now subdued and faded though. Dark. One stripe of yellow-orange split the water from the sky, and a pink blush rippled across the waves.

"Look at the clouds," Navy breathed.

Puffs of pink and gray hung above our heads. "They go on forever," I noted. The sky was larger than life out here. Vast, like you were getting a glimpse of eternity.

The splash of peach and its pink reflection fell back further, until it was a faint wave in the far distance. Before it was swallowed by the gray cold, I fingered the box out of my back pocket.

Swallowing my nerves, I rested my hip on the rail. "I know it might seem crazy, but the way I see it, we only have a week."

She glanced at me, then at the box in my hands. Her forehead slanted in confusion.

"This is for you," I confirmed, inching it toward her.

"Isaiah, I—"

"After our conversation today, I wanted you to know that I meant it, about the kiss. And for no other reason than because I want to, because I like you."

With uncertain fingers, she took it, unwrapped it. I grabbed the paper, crumpled it in my hand, and stuffed it in my pocket. She covered the now obvious jewelry box with her palms and looked up to me, eyes wide.

"I can't accept this, Isaiah."

"Why not?"

"This is a love present."

"It's an intent present," I corrected, pushing her hands, and the box inside, back toward her. "And you don't know what it is yet."

"Well, is it an itty bitty pen?"

"No."

"Exactly."

"Please?"

She shook her head. "I can't promise you anything back."

"I don't want to waste time, Navy. For all I know, we'll never see each other after this week. Open it and let me put it on you." I'd picked it for so many reasons, but mostly this; a necklace would have my hands in her hair.

She squinted at it. "I'm not sure I can."

I went to take it from her and do it myself, but she squeezed it tight. "I'm not ready."

Dropping my hands, I sighed.

We stared at each other. The wind had not died down and her earrings were still dancing, her hair still agitating, her shirt still pressing itself against every curve.

The way I figured it, we were perfect for each other. She wore jeans and white tees every day; I wore jeans and my hat. She lost a dad; I'd lost a dad and a mom. She was a nomad; I was a rancher. Being this was who we were, it was likely we wouldn't see each other again. Of course it didn't hurt that it would help me with my grandma.

"We only have this week," I whispered.

Nestling the box against her chest, she started shaking her head again.

I forced myself to relax. This wasn't a total rejection. It had only been forty-eight hours. "Listen." I glanced to her cupped hands, still pressed against her heart. "Keep it. Think about it, okay?"

At least she was nodding. That was better. How did I keep her nodding?

"Things can stay normal," I tried. The bobs of her head grew faster. "No pressure." They went deeper. "When you're ready, put it on, and I'll know."

"I'm going to, um, I need some time to think, okay?"

"Of course."

"I mean, like, right now."

"Oh. Right. Okay." Of course. She needed time to digest. "You don't want to go peek in the teen lounge for Jesse? Maybe they have movie night again?" Movie night wouldn't be too awkward. You didn't have to talk during movie night.

But she was shaking her head.

"I could text Bern, see if they're together, where they're at?"

"No. No Bern."

And no me, either. That's what she was saying. "I didn't mean to make it awkward." How many times had I said that today? Hopefully only twice.

Shit. I needed to stop making things awkward. That was about the only thing Jesse had on me; he set everyone at ease. That's what I got for being raised in the wild, I guess.

"It's okay," she whispered, not looking like it was very okay. I reached for her hand. She let me squeeze it, even squeezed mine back before pulling away. "But let's, um, I need a little space tonight, okay?"

Gulping down my urge to latch onto her and not let her go, I nodded. I knew what it was like to need some space. I couldn't keep her from that. I could only hope she'd come around.

And quick.

Jesse

Danilo had come to turn down our sheets and set us up for the night, but I'd intercepted him in the hall. When I'd found Dad after finishing my lonely buffet dinner, he'd been passed out on top of his bed already, arms and legs spread like he was making a snow angel but face down.

I didn't want anyone to see him that way.

Danilo was telling me about life in the Philippines, about the vast difference between American excess and what a dollar could buy you in his home village, when Navy came spinning around the corner by the elevators.

Danilo checked over his shoulder for what had distracted me, so both of us were watching as she stumbled toward us, out of breath and in shock. Her hair was tangled, like she'd been in a tornado.

"What's wrong?" I asked, walking the last bit to meet her.

"Miss." Danilo was right behind me. "Can I be of assistance?"

She shook her head, "No, thank you, nothing's wrong. Well, nothing like that. I just, Jesse?"

I wrapped one arm around her and guided her back to my doorway. Danilo and I exchanged a look. I nodded and he nodded back, then hurried off to give us some privacy.

Good guy, that Danilo.

Navy looked like she was waiting for me to open up our room so we could talk in private, but I couldn't do it. And really, no one was ever in the hall for very long, only to walk past and go somewhere. I motioned to the floor and slid my back down the wall. Stretching my legs out, they almost reached the other side.

Navy slumped next to me, and in a rushed mess of words,

explained: sunset, Isaiah, jewelry box, intent. She ended with, "Was that my chance? Should I have let him kiss me?"

"You did say you wanted to be kissed." Freaking sunset too. Freaking cowboy. I shook my head. What was I thinking? My chances were zero to when hell froze over.

But then she rested against me. I tried to relax into it, but my muscles wouldn't cooperate. Like they thought if I moved one bit, I'd ruin it.

"It's such bullshit, you know? He couldn't possibly have done that *for* me, he can't possibly know me enough to be moved by who I am."

"You don't think someone could fall for you in two days?"

"I'm weird-looking."

I snorted. "Nothing about you is weird-looking."

"I have freckles."

"Fairy dust is nothing to be ashamed of."

"I'm not my mom."

"Your mom's a bitch." Shit. I squeezed my eyes shut for a second. "Sorry, I didn't mean that."

Lifting up off me, she said, "No, you're right. I'm so sorry about dinner. It was totally uncalled for. She ran you guys off, and . . ." She shook her head and bit down on her lip. "It was the first thing I should have said, how awful that was. I know I can't apologize for her, but if I could . . ."

She bent her legs up and rested them against my thighs. Her face was serious and apologetic. Clearly, it was important to her that I got the message.

Close up, I could see so much more about her eyes. They were the absolute slightest of browns, a matte bronze maybe, or the color of sand. Not hazel though. Not gold, not green. Warm, soft brown. Screw the sunset, that's what I wanted to see. In and through those eyes.

I did know enough to want more of her and to be moved by who she was. Smart, funny, not inclined to be swayed by what others thought, not trapped by the standards of society, genuine and authentic, comfortable being herself. Plus, she made me feel like I could always be myself, no pretenses. For example, if I bought a stupid hat, she wouldn't hold it against me.

But if she didn't believe Isaiah, why would she believe any of that? Especially when I'd lied to her too.

I hung my head. How could I have lied to her, when she was all that? Not that I'd known then, who or what she'd be. But I knew now.

"It's okay," I finally said, about dinner. "It was my fault."

"How was any of that your fault?"

"My mom doesn't work on a cruise ship," I admitted.

The truth hung between us for a second, and she pulled ever so slightly away from me. Back to square one. I deserved that.

With a deep breath, I explained, "She surprised us with this trip for Father's Day. I thought it was her way of showing my dad how he could make her happy, but then we found out she never bought herself a ticket, because really she wanted to move out when we weren't there."

Ugh. That felt even worse than the lie. No wonder people made shit up sometimes.

Navy furrowed her brow. Yeah, I know, who does that kind of thing, right?

"She left us." I had to force it out. "She's leaving us." *Yes, Jesse, get it through your thick skull.* "That's what's happening right now." Pinching my nose, I let my head drop back with a knock against the wall.

"Wow." Navy let out a short laugh of disbelief, then, "Perhaps, might I suggest, that your mom is also kind of a bitch?"

I closed my eyes. "She didn't used to be."

"Like, before your dad was drinking?"

Letting the back of my head roll along the wall until I was looking at her, I replied, "My dad only started drinking on Saturday."

She sat with that a minute, and I tried to focus on her, rather than the heat that was billowing through my chest. Almost as if she knew I needed privacy before it all spilled out, she went back to resting her head on my shoulder. I squeezed my eyes shut to keep the tears from worming their way out of me.

We sat there, quiet but together, the warmth of her

proximity calming me, for what felt like a very long time.

I opened my eyes when I heard Danilo's familiar shuffle. He met my gaze from ten feet away and I nodded. Closing the rest of the distance to us, he held his palms out, overflowing with the chocolates they put on our pillows each night.

"For the miss," he said. "To make things better."

"Seriously?" Navy pulled away from where she rested against me to reach out for them. "I've been wondering how to get my hands on more of these."

He let them fall into her cupped palms with a smile. "Happy to be of service."

She beamed at him. "Thank you."

"Let me know if I can make your stay better in any other way."

She had a few wrappers open before he'd even turned to walk away, and with three in her mouth at once, she raised a palm to me in offering.

I shook my head. If they made her that happy, I wanted her to have them all. A soft blush filled her cheeks and she stuffed the others in her pockets. Then a bang resonated through the wall behind us, from our bathroom.

I sighed. "I better go check on him. Stay here?"

"It's bedtime really. Plus, aren't you getting up for that glacier viewing in the morning?"

Standing, I admitted, "If I get up early, I'll still only catch the last bit of it."

"Jesse, it's supposed to be amazing. Promise me you'll set an alarm."

I offered her a hand, and when I pulled her up, she stumbled into me. For one brief moment, we were attached, eyes linked, her gasp slamming against mine. Then it was over, and she scooted back to a more appropriate distance.

More noise from our room. Right.

"I'll set an alarm," I promised.

"Good." With the softest, most beautiful smile, she said, "Night, Jesse."

"Night, Navy."

I watched her go, all the way down the long hallway. At the middle, before she turned into the elevator lobby, she caught the wall and looked back. I waved, she disappeared, and I wondered if my dad had already puked in the toilet.

I might as well get to clean up duty now, and crack the patio door before it stunk up the room. Definitely not something I'd leave for Danilo.

Sliding my card in, I slipped into the room and made sure the door was chained behind me. Dad wiped his mouth as he came out of the bathroom, eyes glassy and soul only half there.

You're half there, my mom used to yell at him. Which only made him less there.

"What?" he grunted into my stare.

"You know what," I muttered. Hadn't I already asked him why he was doing this to himself? Shoving by him in the small space, I covered my nose and went to check that he'd flushed. There were only a few splatters, which I had cleaned up in no time. On my way out, I flipped the vent fan.

Thank God there was a vent fan; I'd been in plenty of hotels without one. Closing the door to keep the stink contained and hopefully cycling out, I went to crack open the patio door, then motioned to his bed.

"What, you gonna tuck me in?"

"You have a problem with that?"

"I don't need my son to tuck me in."

"Don't you?"

"I'm doing just fine."

I didn't answer, and he threw himself down on the mattress, pulled the sheet over himself, and rolled to his side. As I covered him with a blanket, he muttered, "Why shouldn't I feel as crappy on the outside as I do on the inside?"

Day 4:

Tracy Arm Fjord, 5:00 a.m. – 9:00 a.m.

Juneau, 12:30 p.m. – 10:00 p.m.

Navy

We were out on our balcony, staring down the rolling face of the Sawyer Glacier. It was early, the announcements that we were entering the Tracy Arm Fjord had woken us before sunrise, and we each had a blanket over our shoulders.

The cruise ship, which had felt massive everywhere we'd been, felt small and insignificant cutting through the narrow fjord. Lush-covered mountains rose up on both sides of us, and waterfalls cut rapidly through their rock faces, rushing down to the clear glass of water below. The sea was the slightest of blues here, a pale cerulean that looked clean and cool and fresh.

And the blue snow cone of glacier that looked to be

squeezing its way through a valley toward us? "Fucking amazing."

"Navy," my mom scolded quietly. "No one's going to kiss you with a mouth like that."

Trying to keep my voice low, I asked, "Do you have a better description for this right now?"

Lowering the camera Guy bought her for their engagement, she wrapped a hand around the long-range lens and offered me a real smile."No, I guess I don't," she admitted.

I hoped Jesse woke up for it. Running my thumb across the screen of my phone, I thought about texting him, but it wasn't really an emergency.

Well, it kind of was, but he'd said he would set an alarm.

We were now at the end of the fjord, facing the glacier straight on, as the cruise ship did an achingly slow 360 to turn around. It was dead quiet, though every balcony I could see had people on it. Something about being in the middle of nowhere, eyes on something you couldn't have thought up yourself, had everyone hushed.

Now I understood why Isaiah was so tight-lipped, if these were the type of mountains—the type of silence—he was used to.

I hadn't opened the box yet. Didn't want to confirm that it was jewelry or think about Isaiah's intent, whatever the hell that was, and what I'd have to pay if I actually noosed it around my neck.

I know, I know, it was my kiss. It felt like it would be a reasonably creepy kiss now, though, because of the box and because of Jesse. My dad might point out that they'd both lied, but Jesse's dishonesty had come out of his own pain, not in order to puff himself up into something he wasn't.

Standing to lean against the railing for one last look of the glacier, I burned it into my memory: a blue-tinged, bumpy, *massive* pile of concrete snow, like it'd been out in the elements for ages, taking hits but never folding.

Maybe that was Isaiah's problem. Maybe he came off gruff and insensitive because he'd been out in the elements for too long, taking hits: a mom who taught him how to lie, the loss of both parents, and the pining after his dad.

But I had to be smarter than my sympathy, for my own sake. Like my mom said, I was highly sensitive, and a feelings collector. So she'd warned me, time and again, not to be swayed by what others wanted of me. *Listen to your brain first, Navy love, and your gut only if your brain is confused. But watch out for what that heart tells you. It's too easily swayed and the moodiest of the bunch.*

"I can't believe how big this thing is," Guy muttered, as my mom kept clicking away at her camera.

It was a rolling hill, flowing through the mountains that surrounded it. The ice blue chunks that had broken off the glacier's massive face were themselves probably as large as a pretty sweet ski-boat.

A blob of something on one of those chunks caught my eye, and I smacked my mom in the arm to get her attention. Grabbing her camera, which was strung around her neck, I yanked her closer to me. Guy was soon cluck-clucking into his binoculars, and I focused the camera until I could see every crisp edge of a seal.

Only he wasn't so crisp. He was kind of a lard actually. But super cute. Light gray and spotted brown. He was on his belly, checking out the boat, and as I clicked pictures, he wiggled his way closer to the edge and slid his flabby form into the sea with a soft plop I could hear from here, because all of us were breathless with wonder.

That's how I wanted to feel after my first kiss, breathless with wonder, and I just didn't think I could get there with Isaiah. Not now, not after everything that had happened. Not when Jesse was standing right in front of me, a better option.

Isaiah

As soon as we were out of Tracy Arm, the morning announcements started: "ATTENTION PASSENGERS: WE ARE DISTRESSED TO INFORM YOU THAT THERE HAS BEEN ANOTHER THEFT ABOARD THE MOONSTAR PRINCE. SECURITY IS NOW MOUNTING A FULL-OUT INVESTIGATION. PLEASE COME TO PASSENGER SERVICES IF YOU HAVE ANY INFORMATION THAT YOU THINK MIGHT BE HELPFUL,

PARTICULARLY ANYTHING SUSPICIOUS YOU MIGHT HAVE SEEN YESTERDAY AT BELOT'S JEWELRY IN THE PIAZZA, OR IF YOU'VE SEEN ANYONE WITH A NEW GOLD AND SAPPHIRE NECKLACE. THANK YOU FOR YOUR COOPERATION AND WE APOLOGIZE PREEMPTIVELY FOR ANY INCONVENIENCE THIS INVESTIGATION MAY HENCEFORTH CAUSE."

Gram paused her make-up application as they outlined the daily schedule, also in our itinerary booklet. "Are you spendin' the day with that Tony boy or comin' with us?"

"Toni is a girl, Gram."

"Well, fine. I'll rephrase." She looked in the mirror at my reflection. "Are you spendin' the day with your boyfriend or comin' with us?"

"I think Navy and I might be starting something."

"Bollocks. That girl looks at Wally's boy like he hung the moon."

I leaned forward in the chair, which was squished in the corner. She was lining her eyes at the mirror along the foot of my bed. "We've had some moments."

"I'll believe it when I see it."

I yanked my hat down further on my head. Did I have the balls to disappear into the crowds of Seattle when we got off the boat? Hitchhike or bus it back to the ranch? If I did, would Gram take me back in the winter when I needed a place? I didn't have enough savings, or any other skills, and didn't know if I could even lease an apartment on my own, being underage.

Taking my hat off, I clutched it in my lap. "I'll go myself, Gram, to the ranch. Buy a bus ticket, hitchhike, whatever it takes."

"You do that, and it will right break my heart. You wanna be responsible for puttin' me in my grave?"

"Don't talk like that."

"You're all I got, Zay. And I'm gettin' old."

I fingered the edge of my hat and sat up straighter. "Then move out to Montana, because I have to go back. You're breaking *my* heart with all this bullshit, don't you see?"

Her reflection pursed its wrinkled raisin lips. "I didn't teach you to feel sorry for yourself."

My dad might have been miserable most of his life, my mom might have been twice as sad because she couldn't make it right, and I might have lost them when I was ten, but Gram always forced my chin up and pointed at the bright side: we had each other, and there would be no more secrets. Everything would be out in the open between us. At least, everything that hadn't been buried with my dad.

I let out a frustrated growl.

Setting her lipstick on the counter, she turned in her seat, prickled. "You got somethin' to say to me?"

"I don't get how you can be such a bigot all of a sudden, when your son—"

"It made him miserable!" Her words came out harsh. She

softened immediately when she saw my face. With a sigh, she whispered, "I'm not being a bigot. I just can't watch what happened to him happen to you."

"But *I'm* not gay!"

"Well." She pulled back like I'd bitten her. "He wasn't either."

I hung my head and tried to loosen the fingers clutching my hat. It might not be disposable, but I was strong enough to crush it if I wasn't careful. "He was, Gram. We both know he was."

"I might know, but you certainly don't," she grumbled.

"I do know. I know you tried to keep it from me and everyone else. I'm sorry you felt like you had to do that. Mom, too. But I'm not Dad. I don't want the ranch because my boyfriend's there. I want it because I need it to survive."

She sputtered. Her eyes went glassy, and she snatched a tissue out of the box next to her. I'd laid it all out and now was her chance to do the same. We'd find a common ground like we always had before, and I'd be shipped back to the ranch as soon as we were off the boat. No need for Navy, no matter how much I ached to bury my face in her hair. There were things more important than girls.

"You've been more and more miserable every time you come home. I see it, just like I seen it with your daddy."

"Because the more you live in a wide open space, the more the noise and bullshit burrow a hole in your head."

We stared at each other. I mapped out her nose, the one I'd inherited from my dad. Her lips, which had shrunk and were no longer the same shape as mine or his. I'd seen him use them on Ike, the owner of the ranch. I'd seen a lot of things I shouldn't have, when we'd been there in the summers. It'd been like seeing into his soul, into the brightest part of it. Gram was right. My dad had been miserable the entirety of his life, except for when he let me see the truth of him there; when he stopped hiding and let himself go.

"Why exactly do you think Dad was miserable?" I asked, all of it finally making a little more sense.

"Because he was gay."

"Because he couldn't live the life he wanted."

"Because he was gay."

"Because you all forced him into a straightjacket!"

"If he hadn't a spent any time at that ranch with that man, he woulda been just fine at home. Everything went downhill for him after that first time he took you out there."

"He was a better dad those weeks at the ranch than he ever was at home. A better man. A better *him*."

"But the rest of the time he was miserable!" Tightening her lips, she shook her head, a quick jerky movement. "That secret, that ranch, that isolation? It ruined him, Zay."

"I know you think you're saving me from his fate, but you're not. You're condemning me to his fate, if you don't let me back there. I promise you, I'll be more miserable *not* going back."

Still shaking her head, she replied, "Ike shoulda known what it was doing to him, and I ain't gonna let him do the same thing to you. I let it go on too long, 'cause I thought it'd help you grieve, but now I'm puttin' my foot down. You ain't goin' back. You're gonna forget that ranch, get used to real life in the real world, maybe get me some great-grandbabies to hold before I die, and I promise you, you'll be happy."

"Do you think me being there is going to make me gay?" I'd never known her to be that ignorant. Please tell me she wasn't that ignorant. "You have to know it doesn't work like that."

"You can tell me the truth, Isaiah. I loved your daddy with everything I had in me, and you know I'll do the same for you."

"You think I'm lying to you?"

She sighed. "Your daddy lied about it until the day he died, no matter how much proof we all had."

"And that's what made him miserable."

"If that's what you think, then stop lyin'."

"But I'm not gay!" And I wasn't my father. Ike might have been his everything, but the mountains were my heartbeat. The horses were the blood that ran through my veins, the back country what lit up my brain. It had nothing to do with secrets and misery. Everything to do with isolation, maybe, because that's who I was. That was me.

She was my mom and my dad and my safety net, yet she was telling me that she wouldn't be satisfied until she forced me into something I was not. Forced me into who she saw me as, instead of letting me be who I was.

"So we're back to this?" I asked. "I prove I'm not gay, and you let me go back to the ranch?"

Hard raps at our stateroom door saved me from telling her that the people who loved you weren't supposed to give ultimatums. They were supposed to understand you. When had she stopped understanding me?

Gram got the door and on the first word of Navy's voice, I jumped up. I'd told her my room was on her floor, a sea view. Flinging myself over Gram's bed to get out, I swung around the corner. "I was just hanging with Gram during the fjord. How'd you know where her room was?" But that was stupid. This room didn't have a window.

Navy straightened to rigid. "*Your* room, you mean? You know, all those lies I thought, well, whatever, but you're the *worst* sort of liar, the kind that never stops."

Throwing a glance over my shoulder to make sure Gram didn't hear that—she was two feet behind me and very interested—I pushed Navy into the hall and closed the door.

"No, Navy, I told you I'm down on your deck, you know? You must have knocked on the wrong door."

"Really? Because Ethel was there, Isaiah, and she told me this is your room. This one. Here."

"You were trying to find me?" I asked.

"Why lie?" She threw her hands up, the jewelry box in one of them. "I don't understand. Make me understand. How do I believe anything else you say? You promised in Ketchikan that it wouldn't happen again, and now here it is, *happening again*. You could have just said, when you opened this door, '*Oh shit, Navy, I forgot I lied about this too.*'"

Dropping my voice, I took a step toward her. "Okay, okay, calm down."

"You know what pisses me off the most? That even after what we've been through on this boat, you still assume I care more about *things*"—she held the box toward the small stall we called a room—"than about honesty and authenticity. Which, coincidentally, you seem to have less and less of." Her face, so tense, like a horse without blinders in the middle of city traffic. "You act like you know me enough to buy me a real gift, but it's only been sixty hours. I could be a serial killer for all you know. I could be the thief!"

"Shh." I tried to reach for her arm, but she jerked it away from me. "Navy, please, I know you're not the thief."

"You know that how? Because you know who is? Because *you are*?" She shoved the jewelry box into my chest. I put my hands up, not willing to catch it, not willing to take it back.

She hadn't had enough time to think. "Please, Navy."

"So you're not denying it?"

"Denying what?"

"Is this the stolen necklace, Isaiah?" She shook it in front of me.

"No! No, no, no, no, no. I bought that in town—"

"It says Belot's, right on the damn box."

"There was a Belot's in town, I swear."

"It matches the description."

"Of course I'd get you sapphires. Your name? I thought it would remind you of this trip, of the sea, of me."

"I don't believe you. Everything has been a lie. *Everything*—all of it."

The door behind us squeaked open. I pushed it back. It popped open again. "You bought her a necklace?" Gram asked through the gap.

I tried to guide Navy down a few feet, away from Gram's ears, but she didn't budge. Instead, she leveled me with a most intimidating stare. "You think he stole it, Liza? Or he use all that money his parents left him?"

"His parents didn't leave him nothin', but he ain't a thief."

Navy shook her head and scoffed. "Of course they didn't."

She cantered down the hall. I rushed after her. "I do have some money. I don't pay rent when I'm there, or food. I've hardly bought anything but this hat. I wanted to spend the rest of it on you. That means something, Navy, it means—"

But the elevator doors closed on me, and my gold reflection was left with a split down its center.

Navy

I flew into Belot's Fine Jewelry. The woman behind the counter gave me a startled look, then one of distrust. She glanced over at an imposing security guard in the corner who uncrossed his arms and stepped toward us.

Pounding the jewelry box down on the table, I pointed to it and said, "Someone gave me this yesterday. I think it might be your missing necklace."

"All information is supposed to be brought to the Passenger Services Desk."

"Please, just tell me if it's the one." I opened it for her and twisted it around so she could see. It was lovely, the pendant a wavy gold coin with the tiniest of sapphire chips near the top right edge.

It was perfect, really. Under other circumstances, I would've loved it.

She shook her head. "We don't sell that one here." Waving the guard back to his spot, her face softened in my direction. "Whoever picked that out has great taste, in jewelry and in girls."

"But this is Belot's," I said. "*You* are Belot's."

She leaned over the gleaming glass counter and whispered, "There's a Belot's at every port."

"You're sure this isn't it? You're positive?"

"The one stolen was bezel set." She pointed to a ruby bezel set in a pair of earrings below us. "It was also snatched off a pad, so there'd be no box." She slid it across the counter and flashed me a smile. "Enjoy it, Love. It's all yours."

Tucking it against my side to both hide it and hug myself, I walked out.

Jesse

"For a minute there, I really thought he did it," Navy said, inching forward in line. We were in Juneau, inside a small white building waiting for the Mount Roberts Tram. Isaiah's necklace might have backfired on him, but he was still all she could talk about.

"At least we aren't suspects this time," I muttered.

"No kidding, right? If it had been the day before, Isaiah and I were there. We went in every store when you were at the piano bar." She frowned. "You think Benoît's going to come after us anyway?"

"No. No way. We were in Ketchikan when it happened." And they knew because we scanned an ID card of sorts every time we got on and off the boat, probably to make sure they didn't leave anyone behind. I guess that meant I could stop worrying about my dad.

"What if it happened after everyone was back, though? It would've been easier then, with more people in the store, more distraction." Her frown went deeper. "Jesse, you left us when we boarded, to find your dad."

It took me a second to realize she was worried about my alibi. I snorted out a short laugh. "You think I did it?"

"No!" Her eyes went wide until I started snickering. She slapped me lightly and I laughed harder. "Of course I don't." She frowned. "But what are you going to say if Benoît asks?"

"Well, I made my dad take a nap, but Danilo could vouch for me. I asked him to bring some coffee for when he woke up." We shuffled forward. "What about you? I'd consider lying for you if you need an alibi, but since I know how you feel about lying . . ."

"I would never ask you to lie for me." Her face was so serious I couldn't help but grin.

"I know, but back to your alibi. Or don't you have one? Are you deflecting, Navy Carmichael?"

She stood up straight, playing along as if she were legit being questioned. "Bern was with me until dinner. We people-watched in the piazza while we had coffee, and then dessert, and then more coffee."

I snickered at her sincere expression and nudged her forward in line.

"What about when you took off during dinner?" she asked. "You have an alibi at the buffet?"

"Ah, but I didn't go to the buffet. That was what I told you, but really I was pulling off the caper of the century."

"Right." She nodded, tone dripping with sarcasm. "I mean, no way they wouldn't have noticed you. Security definitely wouldn't have been keeping an eye on a kid in flip-flops and a hoodie."

I stood taller. "Are you saying that I don't look like the kind of person who could afford a nice necklace for my lady?"

Holding her ticket out to be scanned, she said, "Who would that be? Toni?"

I did the same. "I haven't talked to Toni since you told me how shameful it would be."

We walked up to meet the next half of the line. "Some guys might want a conquest like that," she said. "For a week like this."

"I'm not that kind of guy."

For whatever reason, this slid us into a heavy silence, as if I'd just confessed my undying love and she didn't know what to do with it.

I mean, it wasn't undying, and it wasn't love or anything—I wasn't a total sap—but I did kind of mean it that way. And guessing by how she was chewing on her bottom lip and looking straight ahead, I'm figuring she heard me right.

She sighed out heavily. "Do you think I owe him an apology?"

Back to Isaiah, of course. "My dad always said that if you feel like you owe someone an apology, you probably do." It was the person owed the apology who drank themselves under the table, I guess.

"Except I feel like he'll never stop lying, and that makes me too mad to want to owe him anything."

"But you asked," I pointed out. "So you must feel a little bit like you do."

"Only because I yelled at him. I'm not used to yelling at people."

"I wouldn't mind seeing you yell," I admitted. "Can't quite picture it."

She wrinkled her nose. "You think we'll run into him?"

"Probably." These towns were mostly a small handful of streets. "Did you make plans to meet up with him? I mean, before you got to the yelling?"

She shook her head. "What's Bern doing? Maybe he's with Bern."

"Bern's whale watching."

"How come we're not whale watching?"

"Personally, I don't have the money. You?"

She inched forward again. "Guy stayed back; he doesn't feel good." Looking up at me, she added, "He was in charge of excursions, and my mom is shopping with some of her new Bingo friends."

"Delilah Carmichael does not strike me as the Bingo type." I couldn't imagine her jumping up out of her chair and waving a card in the air. She was pretty contained and measured at all times, as best as I could tell.

"Bingo ladies seem to have an affinity for her favorite hobby."

"Which is?"

"Gossip."

I let out a short laugh as the tram slid into the building and shuddered to a stop. Both sides split open, and as people spilled out one way, those in line filled in from the other.

"How many?" A squat lady in a Mount Roberts polo asked.

"Two," I replied.

She peered into the stuffed cavity, nodded us ahead, then reattached the belt to block everyone else off.

Navy leaned closer and whispered, "Maybe I should've mentioned that I don't like crowds, confined spaces, or heights."

I offered her a hand, a silent I-got-this, and she took it with a hard swallow. Keeping my body between hers and the sardines, I faced her, my back to the people and her back to the sliding door that was sealing its way up.

"I don't want to be by the door," she said, as the tram lurched forward.

Grabbing the rail under the window, I eased us over. The crowd morphed to fill the empty space we left, and once I could rest both hands on the railing, I let go of her fingers to sandwich her between my arms. Her face was millimeters from mine, and she was watching my lips.

The crowd faded out and it was nothing but her face, the minty smell of her, and the view growing behind her head.

"You have to turn around," I told her, though I hated to.

"No."

"You have to see this view." It would make for an awesome tattoo-scape; if only I had a little more time, a camera or sketchpad, and could let go of Navy. Which I wasn't sure I could.

"Is it as good as the glacier?" she asked.

"Half as good."

She squinted a little. "That would be very impressive."

I nodded. "You have to turn around."

"I'm terrified of heights. This is bad enough as it is."

A few strands of hair rested along her cheek, held in place by the sticky gloss on her lips. I wanted to pull them off for her, but knew if I touched her with my fingers my lips wouldn't be far behind. She'd had a rough morning with the necklace confrontation though, and I couldn't be sure yet if she'd really welcome it. Plus, she was clearly uncomfortable in this tram, which wasn't something I could brush off or ignore. And she had to see the view.

Letting go of the rail, I settled my hands on her hips. She closed her eyes—bracing herself because she thought I was going to kiss her, and she had no way out? Like swallowing an anchor, that's how that felt.

Biting my lip so I didn't do anything stupid, I turned her and wrapped my arms tight around her waist. "I've got you. Now open your eyes."

Navy

The mountains were here, back there, and way in the distance, sidestepping each other and the inlet of sea that ran through them. The water was fat and wide, something between a river and a bay, and it wound its way where the mountains allowed it. The peaks were evergreen, dressed with thick masses of pines, and many of them were high enough to be covered with snow. Juneau was nestled between the rise and the water, wherever there was room.

I had one moment to appreciate it before the trees closed in on us and we slid to a stop inside a souvenir shop. They'd laced the space with natural habitat information, but it still smelled like a tourist trap. Opening the door was a bit like Alice in Wonderland though. People, noise, and marketing behind you, but a thick national forest ahead.

The pine trunks rose up bare and gnarled, as if they had faces and souls and stories to share from the thousands of years they'd been there. The ground, rather than flat and full of pine needles, was blanketed with ferns and other low-growing greens. It was dense, hushed wilderness, confined only because of the overgrowth, rather than open like the sea. We walked until I could turn around and see nothing but shades of green over and around and through the gray-brown tree trunks.

My phone vibrated in my pocket, which felt oddly out of place, so I ignored it. Not to mention, I was where I wanted to be: on top of a green-swathed mountain, so rich in texture and color it almost didn't seem real, with the boy I'd finally found who was deserving of my first kiss.

My waist still tingled from where Jesse's hands had been. I'd thought for a second he might kiss me. In fact, I'd hoped that rather than make me look, he'd kiss me instead.

I pick you! I wanted to say, but I'd also been raised a proper lady. And I wanted him to kiss me on his own; I wanted proof he was as caught by me as I was by him.

"Check this little bit of heaven," he said, pointing at a wooden bench. With a beaming smile, he took a seat and threw an arm up along the back. I swallowed as I sat inside it.

Would his fingers dangle to reach my shoulder? Would his arm drop to take me in, instead of the bench? Or would it drop too much, on purpose? No. That would ruin everything. That would ruin him.

It had happened before. Elgin, Illinois, 8th grade: movie theater with new friends, sitting by the funniest boy in class. One hour in, he'd thought my breast was open for the taking, without even trying to kiss me first. I'd elbowed him in the face, giving him a bloody lip and resigning myself to a loner's fate.

We'd moved five months later anyway.

"This is better than whale watching." But I was stiff, trying to keep myself from leaning back too far, into his arm. "You don't need binoculars for this." They were trees, sure, but they had more character than any I'd ever seen, and I felt like we were trespassing. Also, like we were miniatures, dolls pulled from a dollhouse and set out in the real world.

"Where have you seen whales?" he asked.

"California, Hawaii, you know."

"Not really," he said. "We never go anywhere."

I studied him, not sure I should bring it up. "So you thought this was gonna to be, like, a first time family vacation?"

Dropping his head back, he stared at the pinpoints of sky visible through the tips of the trees. "Have you seen the redwoods, if you've been to California?"

I shook my head, taking that as a yes. Yes, he thought this was going to be his first real family vacation. How awful. "I'm so sorry, Jesse. I wish I could do something to make it better."

"You do," he muttered, still looking up. "You have."

I opened my mouth, then closed it; studied the mole under his chin and resisted the urge to press my fingertip against it.

We were nowhere near that familiar, if I was so awkwardly and deliciously charged by the very knowledge of his arm on the bench behind me. I worked my thumb pad over the clear polish on my nails, one by one. My mom had insisted we get our nails done for the trip. I let her pick a color for my toes, but went clear on my hands. I hated nail polish. The chipping and the upkeep. Not worth it.

"These trees are tall," Jesse said. "But those redwoods, someday I hope to see them." He cleared his throat. "What do you want to see next?"

My toes were bright red. The color of kisses, my mom had said. The color of love, I'd thought. I guess that's what I wanted to see next—real love. Not the kind that eventually sent their husband and son off on a cruise so they could pack up and move out, or the type I'd seen men have for my mom that was more adoration and wonder than anything else, but the kind that weathered storms. The kind of love my mom and dad had, the kind she still had for him, even now that he was gone. Because without seeing it, even though she told me about it all the time, I sometimes had to wonder if it truly existed. Or if, had my dad lived, would it have eventually soured like so much else seemed to?

I wiped my sweaty hands on my jeans. "Paris, maybe."

"Yes! And the south of France," he agreed, with the kind of relief that told me he wasn't ready to talk about his mom. "What do they call it?"

"Provence?"

"Proh-*vahnce*?" He tried out the pronunciation, a perfect copy, and I nodded. "You could do both in one trip, right?"

"Sure," I agreed. "On our next vacation, let's go there." The last syllable caught on the potential of his arm though, as he repositioned it against my shoulders. His hand was still a respectable distance away, but he could pull me into him quickly, if he wanted to.

But quick didn't feel like Jesse. No, he'd do it slow, to make sure I was okay with it, to give me plenty of time to change my mind. But I wouldn't. I wouldn't change my mind.

Twisting a little to look at him better, I realized he'd been watching me, and only when my eyes were on him, did he reply, his tone soft and sure and hopeful: "Let's."

The setting couldn't be better. Muffled voices were a backdrop in the distance, but we couldn't actually see anyone else on the path. If I felt it, he must too, right? How could I sense the anticipation that pressed down on us if he were oblivious?

He pulled a strand of hair out of my lip gloss and smoothed it behind my ear. His fingers lingered, and he swallowed hard. I took a deep breath and waited, refusing to look away, refusing to be shy or nervous or act in any way like this would be my first time. But instead of moving his fingers from my hair to my chin, instead of leaning in or pulling me closer, he shot up to his feet.

"Feel like a hike?" But his voice was upbeat and tinny.

I stared at him. "Um, sure?" Was it what I said about his mom? Or too much lip gloss. Maybe he was disgusted by how sticky I might be. It's possible I'd read him wrong, except he'd said so many things, like *how could you think it would be pity* and *you do make it better, you have.*

Wiping my mouth on my shoulder, I stood, following him down the path and further into fantasyland. He was already babbling about the flora and the fauna and the whatever else, and I couldn't help but smile.

Because of course he wouldn't let it be awkward for long.

Jesse

My hand itched to hold hers as we hiked the forest and wandered downtown Juneau.

Literally *itched*.

But she'd looked at me on that bench like she was horrified, eyes so wide and expression so still, like I'd be pushing her into something she wasn't ready for. We'd only known each other a couple days, I couldn't make any assumptions, and I had to be sure it was what she wanted, especially since it was her first kiss. The pressure of that, too, holy subwoofers. Had I been anyone else's first kiss? I didn't think so.

Whatever panic I'd seen on her face though, she'd been planning future vacations with me. Romantic vacations no less; there wasn't a place more romantic than Paris, was there?

So now I sat in our room, waiting for my dad to get ready for dinner, thinking and rethinking over the entire day. What would it have looked like if I'd done it differently?

"What's that for?" my dad asked, pointing to the grin on my face.

I corrected it, and quick. "Nothing."

"That girl you spent all day with?"

"All afternoon."

He gave me a look, the kind that implied he was more sober than he seemed.

"You're not wearing that to dinner, are you?" His jeans had

a dark stain on them, his t-shirt had a hole, and his flip-flops were coming apart.

"Since when do you care what I look like?"

"Since when do you not care?"

He'd always told me that just because a person was inked from head to toe didn't mean they had to perpetuate the stereotype by being messy. It was probably commentary on how he thought I dressed, but still.

"I can't find it in me to care about shit right now, Jess." He stepped over my dress shoes, which Danilo had lined up at the foot of my bed, and opened the door to go.

"Dad, Navy's mom thinks you stole those casino chips, and probably everything else too." I threw a hand in his direction. "This doesn't help. The drinking doesn't help." The not shaving didn't help either, but you could only scold your father so much.

"Who cares what they think. They just lose a wife?"

Brushing past him, I muttered, "Maybe it is you. The kind of drinking you're doing, you probably wouldn't even remember."

"I remember everything," he snapped. "That's the problem."

Spinning around in the hall, I spat, "Mom's not gonna come home to a drunk!"

He laughed, a big belly laugh, like the first time he heard me on the radio. Mom had it recorded. "You think she's comin' home?"

I stammered, caught because I was still working on denial.

He leaned over and set a finger against my sternum. "Listen, kid. I remember everything your mom did to me. I remember and I forgave her, cuz she was my wife. My girl. But now after all that, she can't find it in her to forgive me for being me? Who'd she think she married? I haven't changed. I still put up with her shit. I've always put up with her shit. And what do I get for it?" His voice broke and he dropped his finger. "I get left."

But really, what had happened to him today that he ended up with stains and holes and busted flip-flops? "You need to get yourself together," I said, for the last time. "If not for them"—I pointed at the ceiling, though that's nowhere near where our dinner table was—"then for me, and for her."

With a shake of his head, he brushed past me. "It'll be easier if you face it now, Jess, that she ain't comin' back."

His words hit me like the shriek of acoustic feedback, a noise so screeching and wrong that all the nerves in my brain seized up for one long and awful moment.

Isaiah

Navy had e-ignored me all day. Five texts, none responded to.

"Where's Ethel?" Gram squawked. "She was supposed to be here ten minutes ago."

Shooting up from the bed, I offered to go check on her. Anything to get on Navy's floor.

I raced down the stairs, flew into the hall, glanced both ways to orient myself. Someone was heading into what could be her room. Maybe Guy, judging by the gray-streaked hair.

I waited, in case he was grabbing them for dinner. But no.

Loping the other way, I was at Aunt Ethel's room in no time. Rapping on her door, I squinted down at the other end, praying Navy would emerge.

"Hold up," Ethel called. "One minute!"

Come on, Navy. Text me back, show your face, anything.

The door swung open with a whoosh, exposing Ethel with a hand on her hip. "What's got your panties in a wad?"

"Gram," I corrected. "Gram's panties."

She checked her watch and nodded once. "Let me just get my nice heels on."

"Ethel!" Gram called from down the hall. "What's takin' you so long?"

"Gram, I told you I'd check on her."

"It was gettin' stuffy up there."

I held the door open while Ethel slid on her shoes and reapplied her lipstick. She wiped a smudge off the side of her mouth, patted her hair, grabbed her purse, and joined us in the hall.

"Ten minutes ago, Ethel, you was supposed to be at our room."

"Hush, you. My spa appointment went late."

Gram rolled her eyes. She thought spa appointments made

you soft.

Navy, Navy, Navy, Navy. I couldn't help but chant her name in my head. I'd see her at dinner, but we couldn't talk there. Not with that audience.

Jesse: my rival.

Delilah: the gossip.

Guy: overeager father figure.

Gram: just *waiting* to interrupt and put her two cents in.

Man, Wally was looking like my best friend about now. Maybe I should join him in the bar. Maybe that'd get me some sympathy points.

"Why'd we come back for dinner?" I asked. All we'd done in Juneau was buy me dress clothes for our next fancy meal, but the ship didn't leave till ten. What if Navy was having dinner on the mainland?

"Because Ethel's been alone all day," Gram replied.

"More like you didn't want to pay for a meal that was already paid for," Ethel countered.

We stopped in front of the elevator, and Gram put her hands on her hips. "What's up your butt?"

"I can take care of myself, is all."

"Well I didn't say you couldn't. I just thought it would be nice for you to have some company."

"Maybe I wasn't alone," Ethel snapped. "What do you think of that?"

Jabber, jabber, chomp. Their bickering was amplified in the

elevator. By the time we reached the table, my head hurt.

Hallelujah, though, Navy was there.

I pulled the chair out next to her. She slapped her hand down on the cushion. "This seat is taken."

I sunk onto it, perched at the edge. "Navy, please. I want to talk to you."

"You want your necklace back? I'll get it for you later."

"Of course I don't want the necklace back. It was a gift."

She looked at me. Finally. At least. It felt like I was staring down a horse, convincing it to trust me.

"I'm sorry I accused you," she eventually said. "Okay? I'm sorry I yelled at you."

I nodded, inched a bit closer. "Okay, but I still want to explain."

"What's there to explain?" She sounded weary. "And what's the point? Every time, you've only lied to me more."

I opened my mouth to argue, but she wasn't wrong. That did seem to keep happening.

Hanging my head, resting my hand on top of my hat, I took a deep breath. Weighed the words I wanted to say.

"Leave the girl alone, Zay," Gram said. "And come sit by your granny."

Jesse

My dad was waiting for me outside the Venetian Ballroom. A

silent apology, or maybe I'd struck a nerve and he didn't want to face the judgment alone.

"Took you long enough," he muttered.

In sync, we stepped forward and followed the host to our table. I yanked at my sleeve, cupping a hand over the ink it didn't cover, not that I wasn't proud of it—it was damn fine work. Everyone did their best to ignore our arrival except Navy, who not only smiled, but also softened, her shoulders relaxing as she patted the seat next to her.

Maybe she hadn't been horrified. Maybe she'd just been nervous. I guess looking into the face of a first kiss could do that to a person.

I grinned as I slid into my saved chair.

Balasz was finishing up with Delilah, so I quickly scanned the menu.

"Jesse, sir?" he asked, after Navy ordered. Maybe it should say something to the rest of them, about my character, that I was the only one he called by name.

"The almond harvest soup and the gnocchi please."

As he moved on to my dad, Navy leaned over. "Can I try your soup? I thought about it, but what does almond harvest mean, really?"

"Of course." At least she was here, at this table and on this cruise and part of this vacation. I'd meant it when I told her she made it better. She did. If all I had to do all day was worry about my dad drinking and my mom's radio silence, I might have thrown myself to the seals by now.

"Juneau is beautiful," Delilah cooed. "Guy, you definitely missed out on some amazing vistas."

"As amazing as that glacier?" he asked, leaning over to wink at Navy.

She gave him a tight smile in return, but her mom thought it was hilarious.

"Are you feeling better?" Ethel asked him, unfolding and situating the white cloth napkin in her lap.

"Much, thank you," Guy replied. "I think I just needed to nap off the last of my motion sickness. Now I feel adjusted and much less blurry."

"Motion sickness." Dad snorted. "Maybe that's my problem."

Like a dart piercing the center of the table, that's how it felt when he opened his mouth. Delilah deliberately and with great effort moved her gaze from my dad back to Guy. "I took lots of pictures for you, don't worry."

"Oh, I've seen it before," he assured. "I brought my RV up here a few years ago. Couldn't get to that glacier, but made it all the way up to Anchorage."

"You have an RV?" Navy asked.

"Oh, yes. Guy's a full-time RVer, aren't you, Guy?" Ethel smiled.

"Wait." Navy swung her hair my way to get a better look at Guy. Raising a finger in the air, she continued, "You're a *full-time* RVer?"

"Don't worry, dear." Her mom patted her hand, but she snatched it away as if Delilah's fingers were laced with poison. "You're old enough to stay home without us if we're off somewhere."

"Kansas City was supposed to be about stability, Mom."

"It will be," Guy assured. "Dee made me promise I'd cut back my normal travel schedule. We'll be home at least half the year."

"You don't have to come," Delilah said. "Not all the time at least. I was thinking though, of all the cards we could play. Double Solitaire for hours, while we drive across the country. Or we could have tea and practice your French. Lazy Pineapple Poker, the three of us, and—"

Navy pushed her chair back abruptly, muttered that she was going to the bathroom, and almost took out Balasz on the way.

Isaiah hopped up to follow her. I thought about going too, in case she wanted to be rescued, but that didn't sound like her, and the bathrooms were right outside the dining room entrance. There was plenty of chaos there if she wanted to avoid him.

I ate half of my soup while the rest of them talked about our next port, then slid the bowl onto Navy's empty plate. Balasz always brought out dessert even if we didn't ask for it, and there was a bread basket on the table he didn't let get empty. There was so much food on this boat I was most certainly growing a layer of seal blubber.

But rather than think about Navy and Isaiah making up, I grabbed two more rolls and slid my knife into the butter.

Isaiah

When Navy finally came out of the bathroom, I stepped in front of her, made her look.

"This is like the worst possible time, Isaiah. I am already about to lose it."

"Please, Navy? Hear me out?"

She crossed her arms and pressed her lips together. I'd take that as a yes.

"I just wanna rewind. I'm sorry I gave you the necklace. I'm sorry I said anything. I'm sorry I lied." Lowering my voice, scanning the area for anyone who might overhear, I asked, "I told you about the ranch, right?"

She only stared. Like, duh, you've told everyone about the ranch.

"Okay, so God's honest truth here. Deep dark secrets." I'd never said it out loud and here I was about to tell a girl I'd known for a couple days. But I couldn't see any way around coming clean.

Really clean.

I had to close my eyes to force it out though: "My dad and the owner had this huge love affair. My mom and Gram figured

147

it out and tried to keep it a secret, from me and everyone else. I don't know how stupid they thought I was, but the point is, she doesn't want me going back because she blames him being gay for his depression. Only, he was never happier than when he was there."

Opening my eyes, I let out a shaky sigh. She was listening at least. I could tell by the crease in her forehead.

I continued, "She's afraid I'm falling into some deep, dark hole of misery like he did, and somehow thinks forcing me to prove I'm not gay by getting a girlfriend will make me realize I *am*, or make me realize I want some normal cookie cutter life. Like if I admit I'm gay, I won't need the ranch. Or if I fall in love, I'll want that more than the ranch. So we bet on it: I get a girlfriend, I get the ranch. And she figures if she loses, she'll hopefully still win."

This was a revelation to me as the words came out of my mouth. I stood taller. It hadn't just been a flippant bet like so many of them were. It had been a play.

Navy's forehead narrowed.

Right. But I was here right now. I cleared my throat. "That's why I lied, to get you on my side. So you'd help me win this stupid bet. But it's *not* why I bought you the necklace."

Her expression didn't thaw.

"Well, maybe twenty-five percent why," I admitted. "But fifty percent because of your hair and the other twenty-five because you're pretty awesome. Really, Navy, I like you, I honestly do. I couldn't fake it just for my grandma's sake, I promise."

I waited. She waited. I waited more. That's what I'd had to say. I said it. Now it was her turn.

Finally, she sighed. "How am I supposed to believe that, Isaiah?"

"How can you not believe it? Don't you get how interesting you are, how perfect we are for each other? That's why I bought you the necklace, so you'd know you're special."

"I mean *any of it.*"

My mouth hung open and stalled there. Wait. She was saying she didn't believe my story either, my ranch? Nothing?

Shoulders folding, I took a step toward her and reached for her hand. She kept it tucked in her elbow, and I awkwardly flapped my fingers back to my side. "You're right. I've screwed this all up. I'm telling you the truth though, right now, because I'm begging you to help me. Just pretend even, I don't care. Pretend you like me, pretend we're together, help me show my grandma how into a girl I can be—and I *am*, trust me—so she lets me go back to the ranch. Then you never have to see me again."

She shook her head. "I just don't buy it."

A growl rumbled out of me. "Whatever you want, Navy, okay? It's worth about anything to me."

"I want Jesse."

"Okay, sure. Give me these four days, and I'll make that

happen for you."

"You're so arrogant." She stalked past me. Then, over her shoulder, "Why don't you ask Toni?"

We were halfway through the dining room when I caught her arm and turned her to me. *Last chance. Make it count.* "I don't want to ask Toni."

"The way I see it, you're either still lying through your teeth, or you're only telling me this so you can get back to your ranch. Either way, it's not really about me, is it?"

"Yes! It is! It is about you!" It might have started with wanting access to the mane on her head, but there was nothing not to like about her. We did fit. If I was a normal seventeen-year-old and we lived normal lives at a normal high school, I'd be all about her, for sure.

"But you want the ranch more. And why should I help you, after all the bullshit you've fed me?" Her gaze was steely and came with chills. "You know, maybe if I could believe you had one shred of honesty about you, maybe I'd feel some sort of compassion for your *story* and your cause. But at this point, all everything seems to be, Isaiah, is some new story, some great line, and I refuse to buy it one more time."

Then, jerking away, she took the last of my hope with her.

Jesse

Navy flew back through the dining room, Isaiah in her wake,

working his mouth more than I'd seen him do yet.

Quieting as they hit the table, she slid into her seat while Balasz cleared my soup bowl from her place setting.

"She wanted to try that," I told him.

"It's cold. I will bring a new one."

"I'm okay with cold soup," she said, reaching out for it. "I'm sure it's fine."

"Fine means could be better. I bring better." And he was off.

"Such good service," Guy said. "The one place you can still count on it." But it seemed Navy was ignoring him now too.

"Come on," Delilah said, trying to grab hold of Navy's chin. "Don't be upset about this." But when Navy wrenched her face away, her mother frowned. "It'll be good for you, to spend some time alone."

"Normal mothers would worry about their teenager being alone," Navy muttered. "Parties and *kissing* and stuff. Think of all the things I could do."

"But you won't, because you're you."

"Being highly sensitive doesn't mean I always make good choices," she hissed.

"It means you're too careful. And skittish. And you think everything through."

"There's nothing wrong with having a plan and not making rash decisions."

"See?" Delilah patted Navy's hand with a grin. "You'll be just fine."

Navy made a fist and pulled her hand into her lap.

The table was very interested in their conversation, but I might've been the only one who could actually hear them. It felt wrong though, all those eyes on a private argument.

"There's a mocktail dance party in the teen lounge tonight," I said.

Navy eked out a bare smile, thin and tired. "Whatever you want, Jess."

Isaiah stabbed his salad with a knife and snaked lettuce off the end of it with his tongue.

I snorted out a short laugh. "I know that's how you feel about the teen lounge, dude, but it's kind of creepy."

He tossed the knife onto his plate with a clang and threw his arms up. "I don't have a fork."

Grabbing my dessert fork, I handed it across the table to him.

"You know what I was thinking?" He sneered while he grabbed for it. "I was thinking Wally here isn't with it enough to pull off any great heists, but Jesse sure is."

I choked on my water.

"What?" Navy snapped.

Cocking his head to the side, he said, "Yeah. Always sticking his nose in everything. Talking to everyone. Playing up what an easy-going guy he is? Great alibi. Who knows, maybe he's going to throw his dad under the bus at the end of the week. Maybe it's working out just perfect for him."

Dad leaned back in his chair, curious to see where this was going, but I was too shocked to answer.

Navy placed her palms on the edge of the table and leaned over. "How dare you drag him into this."

"Into what?" Isaiah asked, as if he was simply making conversation.

"You don't assassinate someone else's character because you don't like what's been revealed about your own."

"I might be a liar, but I'm not a thief."

Clamping a hand on my thigh, Navy squeezed with all her might. "Why do you never defend yourself?"

It took me a beat to realize she was talking to me. I pointed at my chest, just to be sure.

"Yes, you," she snapped.

"I have no idea what to say," I admitted. "I thought we were friends. All of us."

Isaiah's aunt and grandma sat silent, Guy couldn't stop nodding, and Delilah elbowed Navy on her other side. "You've really started something, haven't you?"

As if that was a good thing.

Isaiah

After tucking my tail between my legs and busting out of dinner so I didn't make more of an ass of myself, I holed up in our room to research a job that didn't make me want to jab a pen through my ear.

I'd taken affinity tests with my thumb. Aptitude tests. Stupid-of-course-this-isn't-going-to-tell-you-anything tests. Each one said I should be a park ranger. Or a fisherman. Or, essentially, an effing stable hand.

Unfortunately for Gram, it had never been so clear that I wouldn't fit in any other box but my own. Which meant it was time to work on Plan B.

Thinking Aunt Ethel might have some ideas, I hurried down to her room. I still had her spare key, which I'd borrowed when pretending it was my room, but I knocked anyway.

The door swung open quickly, and her smile tilted when she saw me. "Oh. Hey, Zay."

Both sides of her bed were mussed. A teacup sat on the opposite side table from her book, reading glasses, and coffee mug.

With a snort, the question spilled out, "You didn't go to the spa today, did you?"

"Keep this between you and me, okay? That grandmother of yours has a big mouth. I don't need people judging me."

I sat down with a grin. "Way to go, Aunt Ethel."

She waved it off. "What's up?"

Leaning back in the chair, I took off my hat and ran a hand through my hair. "I thought maybe you'd have an idea of what I'd like besides the ranch."

"Girls?"

"I mean a job."

She snickered. "Right, of course."

"Or I thought you could talk some sense into Gram."

"She told me about your conversation today."

"Yeah, pointless."

Tapping her red fingernails against the table, she said, "I'm sorry you were caught in the middle of all that."

"Help me. Please?"

"Your gram is stubborn as a tick. She doesn't let go of something without Vaseline and tweezers, and even then, she'll leave something behind for you to remember it by."

"But so am I," I pointed out. "And so are you. And you make *sense* when you talk. And she's more likely to listen to you."

She patted my hand a few times, pulled back, settled into her seat again. "It's not like I haven't been trying."

I flicked my nail at the edge of the table while she took lotion out of her purse to spread over her hands and elbows. Expensive lotion she'd been ordering from Italy since her first trip there. So far, she hadn't brought me out of the country, but she kept saying next summer, for my eighteenth.

"How about don't take me on a birthday trip, or any trip at all. Give me that money instead for my off-season rent, and I can manage the rest." I nodded. There was a plan. And long-term too.

Recapping her lotion, she sighed. "I told one person about your daddy, and Liza didn't talk to me for five years. I'm sorry I can't fix this for you, Zay, but I'm not making the same mistake again, helping you do something she doesn't want. It's time for you to fix your own problems. Be a man and all that." Pressing her lips together, she added, "Ten months and you're an adult anyway, then you can do what you want."

Ten months felt like a lifetime. I'd be swallowed up in ten months without the ranch. I could no longer blame my dad for how he let the rest of his life slip away. I understood. I could see how quickly it might happen.

"Isaiah, I have to ask you something, right now and quickly."

"I'm not gay."

Waving her hand, she leaned back. "No. Not that. I don't care what you are. Listen, I trust you, and I never would ask you this, except for the fact that you just came to me for money. I mean, I guess you wouldn't have asked if you'd already taken it, but you haven't helped yourself to anything from my safe, have you?"

"What?"

A knock at the door interrupted us. She jumped to answer it. Was my aunt getting a booty call twice in one day?

Benoît? *Benoît* was her booty call?

"Bonjour, Madame," he said, without a glance in my direction. "You have a theft to report?"

Duh. Of course. He was probably only in his late twenties. I almost laughed, that something between them was my first thought, rather than—wait, what?

"It had to be that room attendant of mine," she said.

Isaiah

I paced the hall in front of the teen lounge, not willing to face Navy and Jesse without Bern. Without something soft to stick between us if they started throwing punches. Not that I didn't deserve them.

The gold doors dinged open. Bern hopped out and raised his hands. "Mocktail dance party!" While beatboxing a bit, he jerked his body in what might have been considered some sort of dance move.

I squeezed out a smile, since that seemed to be what he lived for, then told him what went down at dinner. How now, in light of Ethel's news, it couldn't have been Jesse.

He whistled. "You dug your own manure pile there, Cowboy."

"They're going to think I'm only sorry because there's proof he didn't do it."

"Which is true, correct?"

I didn't reply. Navy did the same with the necklace, though. So there.

"Listen." He clapped me on the shoulder. "Decent humans apologize when they need to apologize, no matter the circumstance."

I bristled. "I'm a decent human." But I couldn't help but

wonder. What did I know about humans, really? The normal kind who interacted with lots of people on a regular basis. Who weren't pulled in a million directions that dictated their truths and behaviors first, before considering what was right?

I closed my eyes, tried to center. This ship and its noise had me all twisted. I couldn't think straight. That was the problem here. That's why I kept screwing up. Or at least that's what I was going to tell myself.

What was currently wrong? Everything. But most recently? I'd attacked an innocent rabbit. No matter what else, I needed to straighten that out.

"Okay, I'm ready."

Bern nodded, then guided me into the darker than normal room. The sea stretched for miles outside. Serene. Inside though, it was loud music, a disco ball, and long tables lined up as a makeshift bar. This ship was too much, all the time. Overstimulation.

Navy and Jesse were laughing, pouring juice and soda into a cup from both sides.

She froze when she saw us, eyed me like I was a vulture. So fine. My outburst at dinner was stupid and immature. I'd lost it. I couldn't help it. The way she'd been looking at him, like he could do no wrong. Like she'd follow him anywhere, even to the teen lounge.

"Whatcha got there?" Bern asked, sticking his nose between them.

Navy's disc earrings shook as she offered him the cup. "Wanna try?"

"Wait." Bern put a finger in the air. "Is Navy Carmichael sharing germs?"

She shot a glance at Jesse. "I guess I am."

Bern took the cup and drained it while rubbing a hand on his stomach. Were Navy and Jesse more together than I knew? Of course they were. They'd probably been making out all day. I was a complete idiot. Why else wouldn't she have answered my texts?

Toni came up behind Jesse and squeezed his sides. He startled, jumping into Navy, who caught his elbow with her hand.

"Hi y'all! We're officially starting! Gather in teams and work on that mocktail! When you're done, bring it over to the judge's table!" She hopped to the next group and said it again.

"I'm sorry, Jesse," I blurted out. "I don't know what got into me."

They all looked at me. Like I didn't mean it. Or like that was the worst apology they'd ever heard. I glanced at Bern, who jerked his head away like I was supposed to take Jesse somewhere private and do it right. But then Navy wouldn't see it.

It's what a decent human would do, though.

I *was* a decent human.

"Can we talk?" I asked him. "In the hall maybe?"

He set the cup down on the table. "Sure, man."

Of course. Because no matter what abuse he took, he didn't have any problem being a decent human.

It was infuriating.

Once in the brighter hall, I tried again. "That was uncalled for. At dinner. Shit, maybe I'm losing it. It wouldn't surprise me. Anyway, you didn't deserve it."

He rubbed at the tattoo on his elbow. "It's not me, and it's not my dad."

"I know. I know, okay?"

With still fingers now, he nodded. "As long as you know."

"I do." We stared at each other. "I do because my aunt's missing money from her safe, and obviously neither of you have been in her room."

He smirked. Like he knew the apology wouldn't have come otherwise. It would have though. Whatever.

"So the bandit strikes again?"

I nodded. "The bandit strikes again."

With a grin, he motioned for Bern and Navy to join us, then filled them in.

"Is this like, more theft for real?" Bern asked. "Or she's kind of kooky and misplaced it?"

"She thinks it was her room attendant. Danny or something?"

"Danilo?" Jesse asked.

"Sure, probably."

"No." His voice went cold and monotone. More than when he'd been in trouble. "He would not jeopardize his job like that, not when his mom is sick."

"How you get to the heart of people so quick is some sort of voodoo magic trick," Navy muttered, but with pride.

"Is she supposed to forget a thousand dollars?" I asked.

"Maybe it's you." Navy squared her body to stare at me straight on. "You did try to deflect the blame at dinner."

"What?"

"Yeah, how's that feel? Maybe it's you. Who else is in her room, pretending it's theirs? Who else has so much access?"

Bern snapped his fingers in the middle of our circle. "Enough. We are not going to fight. We love each other. It's the four of us until the end." Into his shoulder, he muttered, "Of this trip."

Jesse put a hand on Navy's arm. They shared a look. "It's cool," Jesse whispered. "Isaiah's cool."

This is what soothed her. Softened her. To me. He fixed what I couldn't.

"Danilo," I snapped. "Danilo is the only one with access. She doesn't even lock it."

"Okay," she said, now soothing me. "Okay."

"It's not Danilo," Jesse insisted. "He makes plenty of money to support, like, his entire family."

"Well, no one else has been in her room when she wasn't there."

Jesse moved toward the stairs. "I have to find him, give him a heads up."

We watched the empty space he'd left, till we could no longer hear his feet pounding the steps.

It didn't take long, considering the music in the teen lounge. Bern frowned. "So no mocktail dance party?"

Navy bit at her lip. "We should go with him, shouldn't we?"

"There's nothing we can do," I said, even as she was walking away. I had bigger problems than Navy though.

I needed a plan C.

Jesse

Benoît looked up as I turned the corner. Of course.

Bruiser had Danilo by the arm, and Danilo was blabbering incoherently, obviously confused, the same way I'd been when they'd come at me.

"He didn't do it!" I called, hurrying forward to meet them at the service elevator before they could disappear.

Danilo quieted as they turned their attention to me.

"You seem to be saying that a lot," Benoît said, exchanging glances with Bruiser.

"It couldn't be him," I insisted. But it sounded weak even to me. What was I doing, rushing to fix things that couldn't be fixed?

"You've known him awhile?" Benoît asked, though his tone

162

implied he knew very well I hadn't.

Okay, yeah, there'd been a lot of that too.

"Or you know he didn't do it, because you did?"

"No!" *Shit.* I ran my hand through my hair and tugged at the ends. "I didn't do it, and of course I just met him, but he wouldn't do this. I get gut feelings about people and—"

Benoît grabbed my arm and pressed the button.

I tried to step back, but even though he was short, he was sturdy as hell. Sturdier than me, that was for sure. "I didn't do anything, you don't have reason to take me anywhere, you can't just take people—"

Bruiser narrowed a stare in my direction as the door opened, this one without any ding. "You know something was stolen, and it hasn't been announced yet."

My heart flew into arrhythmia, or at least as close as it had ever gotten to arrhythmia. Did arrhythmia make people want to cry? "No, listen," I forced it out, a pathetic breathless whimper. Gah, why did I have to sound so guilty? Straightening, I took a deep breath and tried to compose myself. "My friend, you know, the guy with the cowboy hat? It was his aunt, so of course I know, I—"

Benoît cut me off with a jerk into the elevator. "Another connection you have to yet another victim, Jesse Kowalski. You are now an official suspect."

Navy

The elevator stopped at nearly every deck. Impatient, I slipped out with a Polynesian family, Hawaiian lilts to their A's, and took the stairs instead.

My floor—Ethel's floor—was empty, but I caught them on Jesse's. He, Benoît, Bruiser and a man in room attendant attire disappeared into a hole in the wall, an elevator I'd never noticed before. Running the last leg, I made it as the doors began to close.

Benoît sighed as I burst into the space. "Mademoiselle, you are not to be on this elevator."

"I'm here for Jesse," I said, aiming for calm and professional, polite but reserved. Why was Benoît's arm on him like that? "And nice to see you again, Benoît. I can assure you there's been some sort of mistake." I motioned toward the room attendant, whose name I didn't remember. "If Jesse trusts him, I trust him."

"This matters nothing."

Bruiser grunted. "We may not be a crack operation, but do they really think we're that stupid?"

Benoît chuckled. "Guilt makes people crazy sometimes."

"We're not guilty," Jesse and I chorused.

The elevator shuddered to a stop, definitely not the smooth ride of the gilded version, and the doors wobbled open. Benoît dragged Jesse out, and Bruiser guided the room attendant into the hall. Though the dingy white walls on this level looked teeming with germs and puss-filled infections, I forced myself out of the elevator.

Hugging myself to keep from contamination, I followed them down a narrow hallway into a graying room with three doors. A table and four chairs were pushed to the side, next to a little fridge and a coffee pot on a crate.

Bruiser locked the attendant in one room, while Benoît shoved Jesse into the other. Gripping a chair by its back, Benoît dragged it into the hallway and pointed. "Sit here, or go away."

The door swung shut behind him, and sealed itself into the wall the same as any of the others. There was nothing official about the room or the door they'd chosen, and I'd never be able to find my way back if you spun me around and took the chair from its post.

Toeing it farther from the wall, I twisted my hair up in a bun so it couldn't touch anything and sat.

Everything creaked down here, and my phone wasn't working. No bars, no service. It was sluggish at best, drunk off the distance from any real-world contact. I couldn't text Jesse and ask for his dad's info, and I couldn't call my mom for help.

All I could do was wait.

Jesse

Bruiser handed me a soda and sat down with a grunt. Water

lapped against the tiny porthole almost as frantically as my heart thrummed against my ribcage.

"You were not officially near the first victim in the camera roll," he said. "But you could have snagged the purse, skipped the line, got your picture taken, and slipped on board."

"I did not skip the line." Gripping the can, I focused on its temperature. It reminded me to be ice cold. Cool. Calm and collected.

"You said in your stateroom yesterday that you skipped the line."

"No, I said—"

"Arguing with law enforcement over semantics does not make a person look innocent."

I snapped my teeth together, but not defending myself didn't feel very good either.

"You and your dad were in the bar when the second victim lost his chips."

"Untrue. I wasn't there *when* it happened, and my dad has the bartender as an alibi."

He squinted at me. "You know when it happened, because you did it?"

"No, I mean, I—"

"Your dad did not leave the boat yesterday, at all, and you bought a muffin in the piazza around the time the necklace went missing."

This time I didn't reply, since he wasn't listening anyway,

but he waited until I couldn't stand it any longer. "Have you seen the size of those muffins? They take awhile to eat. That's my alibi. Plus, *I didn't steal the necklace.*"

"Which brings us to the present moment, where you know inside information before the rest of the boat has been notified, and seem far too involved in all this to be merely an innocent bystander."

That I had no argument for. I opened the can of soda and downed half of it in one gulp.

"I mean, I get it. Cute girl chasing after you? You want to be the big man, buy her stuff, show her a good time."

Resting the can on my knee, I tried to stay calm. "You're not even asking any questions."

"I'm working out your motive."

"That's not my motive. And you can't have any proof." But I was more reminding myself than talking to him.

Bruiser leaned back in his chair. "We're bringing the victims down to ID Danilo. Might as well have you around for that too, since you're everywhere you shouldn't be."

Setting my elbows on my thighs, I clasped both hands around the soda: *be cool.* "Listen, I didn't skip the line, I have two to four alibis for the casino chip incident, and I met up with Navy immediately after buying the muffin. On top of that, I don't know what room the money was stolen from. Plus, I was in Juneau till dinner, then went straight to the teen lounge, which is when I heard about it. So, all sorts of alibis for yesterday. It wasn't me."

"But was it your father?"

"No."

"How can you be sure? Are you more sure about your father or your room attendant?"

"Both."

He crossed his arms.

Ugh. Fine. "My father, of course."

"Listen, if nobody IDs you, you're free to go. But don't think I won't be watching you from every camera we have on board. If I find out you're lying to me, or if you do one thing remotely suspicious, I'll slap as many fines on you as I can, maybe a night in jail to top it off. If nothing else, you will no longer be welcome on any of our future cruises. Got it?"

I gulped down his threat with a few solid swallows. He was staring at me, waiting to see how my innocence or guilt would respond, so I forced out the slightest of nods.

There was a knock at the door and he stood to leave. From the slice of the room I could see as the door swung open, Navy was no longer waiting for me.

Navy

I jumped when the door opened next, but Benoît didn't glance at me as he strode out of the room.

He disappeared into the elevator, and I paced the length of

the hall. At the end, by the singular, suffocating window, I finally had some service. One small dot of a bar, but it would have to do.

I almost texted my mom to find Jesse's dad, but then didn't want her thinking any worse of him than she already did. So I texted Jesse for his dad's number, but that was stupid because if he had service he could contact him himself. Bern wouldn't know where to look or even what Wally looked like probably, since he wasn't at our dinner table, but I gave him Jesse's room number so he could at least go knock. Though, at this time of day, if Wally was in there, he most likely wouldn't be awake to hear anyone at the door. I could ask Isaiah, but he was maybe too close to it, too close to his aunt.

Benoît had said that Isaiah was near the first victim in line, and we hadn't been with him until noon the day the casino chips were stolen. As for the necklace, we hadn't seen him once we were back on the ship until dinner, so, if it happened in the afternoon, he would've had plenty of time to steal it. Maybe buying one in town was a ploy, to throw everyone off, because if you bought one, why would you also steal one?

Casino chips wouldn't do anything for him, though. He couldn't cash them in; he wasn't eighteen. Unless they didn't bother checking your ID when cashing them out, assuming someone had already verified your age when you'd gotten them in the first place.

And his aunt's money would be easy. Or maybe that was

him, and the rest someone else. He could be using the suspicion for cover. Blaming Jesse would make sense too. I wouldn't put anything past him at this point. If he wanted back on the ranch bad enough—which was obvious—and he didn't have the strongest morals—also obvious—and his grandma wouldn't help him get there, and he had no money, then maybe this was how he planned to do it.

I sat back down in the chair as the doors on the elevator opened. Benoît emerged with a gaggle of geese trailing behind him: two old ladies, the jewelry saleswoman I'd talked to earlier, and Ethel. They swept past me as Benoît ushered them into the room. Ethel hung back a moment to eye me, confused.

But I was too occupied with one of the little old ladies to care. I recognized her, but from where?

Jesse

After what felt like fifty-five million years, during which my insides drained away and left behind a panicked sort of reverb—pulsing and steady, hot and suffocating—Benoît opened the door and held it wide. "None of the victims recognized you, except the lady who sits at your table, like you said. And since we've already searched your room, you're free to go."

I didn't move. It was hard to believe him.

"Not that I won't be watching you."

Okay, that was more like it. I stood, and he offered to take my empty soda can. It felt like a test, like what would it say about my character if I handed someone else my garbage? No thank you, I would get rid of it myself.

No one was in the next room. No old ladies, no Ethel, no Navy. Only Bruiser and Benoît.

"What's going to happen to Danilo?"

"None of your business."

"But he's my friend."

"You made lots of friends in these few days. Perhaps you should be more picky."

"He wouldn't have been in the piazza." The workers seemed to get to their posts mysteriously, as if they vanished in and out of thin air. Probably via the service elevators, but still, I had never seen Balasz or Danilo wandering around, enjoying the ship, and I was almost positive that was on purpose, that it wasn't for them, that they weren't supposed to mingle.

Only Toni and the coordinators, because they set up dinners for the teens in the buffet and pulled food for the lounge upstairs.

"And he couldn't have been in line. You guys were all on board already, weren't you?"

"Let us worry about that, Jesse Kowalski, and try to enjoy the rest of your vacation. Maybe we will not have to meet again, hmm?"

"I bet you'd tell Navy, if she were here," I muttered,

slumping my shoulders.

He frowned and motioned out the next door, the one that led to the hallway. "She might have understood me."

I shot out of it and nearly tumbled over her, on a chair by the door. I wanted to cling to her for staying, for still believing in me after the hour I'd spent doubting myself. It was amazing the kind of guilt a guy like Bruiser could make you feel, even when you knew you hadn't done anything wrong. With a smile of relief, she stood. And without missing a beat, she reached for my hand.

"You okay?"

"What're they doing to Danilo?"

"No one recognized him besides Ethel, and they didn't find anything in his room."

"So he's cleared?"

"He's on probation and confined to his room. They're trying to find out who might be hiding the stuff for him, and until they get more proof either way, he won't be working and he won't be paid."

"How do you know all this?"

"Benoît told me in French. I don't think he figured I could keep up with him, American that I am, but I did. I can." A smile bloomed on her face, and I pulled her into a hug. She'd stayed. She sat in this gross hall on this stained and gummed-up chair in what might as well have been a sewage tube underwater, and she'd done it for me.

She had chosen me. And not just because Isaiah fumbled.

Isaiah

The announcements pricked at my consciousness, but it was the movement of the boat woke me. Like I was breaking a horse.

It was pitch black outside. Definitely not morning. Gram still snored lightly from the other side of the small room.

My phone whirred on the nightstand. Propping myself up, I reached for it. It was midnight. Bern was with Jesse and they wanted Navy and me awake. The ship had gone off course into a storm. On purpose, to save a yacht.

Another text. Bern saying he wouldn't stop until he saw my shining, dimpled face in his room.

Pulling on the jeans I'd left crumpled by the bed, I grabbed a long sleeve flannel for over my tee. Phone, keycard, boots. The hat could stay behind.

It must've been some storm, because it was the first I could tell that the ship was moving, aside from being at the pool and watching the water move. Bracing myself on the wall, I left quietly and staggered down the hall for the stairs. Navy was coming up them in pajama pants, her hair mussed like frayed hay. Ears bare, infinity necklace around her neck, no lip gloss, black tee.

She'd worn white every day. They hadn't all been the same

shape, but they'd all been the same color. The boat rocked, and I grabbed for the rail. She eyed it like it would bite.

We took the next step simultaneously, and again the boat repositioned itself, almost sending us into each other.

"I was dreaming that I'd never see you again," she said, her voice soft and sleepy. "You were standing on top of a mountain that no one could get to. There was a fire and a horse and a bear carcass, and I had, like, the sight of God to even see you there, because you were surrounded by mountains and mountains and seas, and *no one* could get to you."

"Doesn't sound so bad, actually."

"Right. So what do I care if you're still lying to me or not? I'll never see you again."

I frowned. "But I'm not."

She stumbled ahead of me down the hall. Fists out against the walls in case she needed to brace herself. No reply.

"I'm sorry I've been hounding you so much," I said, trying on the decent human saddle one more time.

"Nothing you say is going to make me want to help you, Isaiah."

"I don't want you to help me. I want a redo."

She stopped and turned.

"I swear." Putting a hand out to shake on it, I added, "Let's start over."

She studied me, sighed. Rolled her eyes. Slid her palm against mine. "Fine. I accept your truce."

As we neared the number Bern had texted me, uniformed ship employees spilled out of the utility elevator. They split up to knock on doors:

"Everyone must stay inside," they said.

"No balcony use."

"Turn the lights off, please."

"Yes, all the lights, not just balcony lights."

"No cameras."

"No *flash*," they emphasized.

"Close balcony doors, stay inside."

One pointed at me. "Sir, you'll tell them?"

Jesse flung open the door and grabbed Navy's hand to pull her in.

I nodded at the uniforms and slipped into Bern's room. They were, in fact, all on the balcony, which was lit up. A girl who must have been Bern's sister was taking pictures.

"They're telling everyone to turn off their lights, stay inside, and not take any pictures," I said.

"Oh, I got some good ones," the girl said. She had the same thick hair that Bern did. Same swoop up and off the forehead, only hers fell to her chin.

His dad stood. Flicking the lights off, he lurched us into darkness. Spotlights from a helicopter above searched the sea, but before I could get a good look at anything, Bern's mom was ushering us inside.

"Let's go up to that piano bar on the piazza deck," Jesse

suggested. "Those booths right against the windows?"

And without a word, the four of them were out the door, half on top of each other. But I didn't run unless there was a barn on fire.

Navy

Jesse let me sit by the window, Bern and his sister slid in across from us, and Isaiah slipped into the booth behind with a not-so-graceful sounding slide.

The piano lounge and the entirety of the piazza were dark. "This seems prime for another theft," I said.

I'd left Jesse with Bern in the teen lounge before I'd gone to bed, because at least security would trust the coordinators for an alibi. Now we were in the dark and back at the scene of a previous crime.

Pressing my forehead to the glass, I tried to get a glimpse of the yacht we were supposedly rescuing. It was buried down there, in the agitated swells that were erratically pitching the massive ship, and a helicopter above was haphazardly skipping its light back and forth. I could only see what it illuminated, and it was having a harder time staying steady than we were. If it weren't for Jesse's foot braced on the outside of the booth, we probably would've slipped out.

I couldn't imagine what it had to be like for that little yacht. I'd be flat terrified and out of my mind.

"Toni says we'd never sail into a storm like this, but we were the closest to them. Coast guard and human decency and all that."

Jesse's thumbs worked across his phone, and I tried not to pout. After everything—after today—he was still texting her? "I thought you weren't supposed to use your phone."

He glanced up and explained, "She's keeping tabs on Danilo for me. Making sure Benoît's being nice about it. Plus, I'd consider this an emergency."

"Look!" Bern's sister tapped her finger against the window.

Four burly guys came down the walkway that circled the ship, gearing up to head down in a lifeboat. "A *lifeboat*?" I cried. "They'll get swallowed out there!"

"They're trained for it," Jesse said, attention back on his phone. "They train for rescues."

"That what Toni says?" I muttered.

"Yes." It was a husky whisper into my ear, and the heat sent a shiver down my spine. "That's what Toni says."

I snapped my head around. Was he playing with me? But his face was soft and focused on me now. Like I could have his attention anytime I wanted it, and he was making sure I knew.

Breaking eye contact first, I went back to the guys snapping and clipping and donning gear.

Jesse's phone beeped again. "Coast Guard didn't think they could get the helicopters here, were worried about it being too windy for them, but now that they made it, they probably won't need our guys. They're just in case. Now they want us to block the wind so it's easier for the copters to get in."

The bartender beyond the piano, lit by the very low lights of the alcohol case on the wall behind him, was flying here and there to catch things as they rolled—things that had indents to keep them in place. Indents be damned, apparently, in a real storm.

"Their rudder busted, so they couldn't navigate. It's a couple and a dog."

"Can you imagine being out in the middle of this?" Bern's sister asked. "No one around? They had to think they were going to die."

Silence fell as we watched the beam try to center on the yacht, as the copter tried to stabilize itself, as the cruise ship attempted to both stay out of the way of the copter and close enough that it was blocking any wind.

"What would you be thinking right now, if it were you out there?" Bern asked.

"I'd be praying," I whispered. "Like a good little pastor's daughter."

"Your dad was a pastor?" Jesse asked, surprise in his voice.

I nodded, my attention on the inky blots of torturous waves.

"Your mom was married to a pastor?" Isaiah asked.

"What's that supposed to mean?" I snapped.

No one said anything, and I couldn't really blame them. It was like she'd been trying to forget by avoiding everything he was. She'd searched so hard to fall in love again, and failed so many times, it made sense she filled herself with other things now—with vanity, and gossip, and a long string of engagements.

I shook my head. How could I miss someone I never really knew? Maybe it would be worse to be Isaiah, to have known and lost, than to not have known at all. Or Jesse—how would it feel if my dad had been around all this time and was now choosing to walk away and ignore my calls?

It would be awful. Unimaginable. I'm not sure I'd have it in me to care about anything or anyone else. And yet here Jesse was, still trying to stick up for people, putting his neck on the line to save Danilo, a guy he'd just met.

He made me want to be better, as best I could, as good and pure as him.

Jesse

Two hours into the rescue and Navy was settled against me, dozing off. The scent of her floated about—fresh but natural, feminine but nothing fancy. No perfumes, no strong shampoo. Just girl. Just Navy.

As she sunk deeper into sleep and harder against my chest, I wrapped my arms around her to keep her from falling and hitting her head on the table.

She was, I decided then, the most authentic person I'd yet

met. She'd never once apologized for having space or germ issues. She didn't blink when she said she went to sleep early. All the things my friends back home would try to hide, and she didn't hide anything. She made me want to be that authentic too. She made me want to live up to her, to who she deserved, longer than for the rest of the week, because I would never forget her. I couldn't. I didn't want to.

Toni kept texting me and I was trying to ignore it. I wanted to be here right now, exactly here, at the expense of these poor people who were on the edge of a sinking ship.

Shake it off, Jesse. This is not about you and Navy. This is about death's door.

"Look." Isaiah pointed to the Coast Guard rappelling from the copter. The wind was swinging the copter, and swinging him, and swinging his targets, and swinging us.

"Navy," I whispered, shaking her a little. "Navy, wake up. This might be it."

"Hmmm?"

"It's almost over. Wake up."

She shifted onto her hip and nuzzled her face into my chest. I gathered a chunk of her hair with my hand and let my fingers trail down it. Isaiah caught my eye and his nostril flared.

My stomach was rock solid but even I could feel it tonight, my gut shifting with the boat's movement.

Resting my mouth against the skin of her ear, her actual soft skin, I whispered. "Wake up, Midnight. Time to wake up."

"NAVY!" Bern shouted, and she jumped.

"What?" Looking around, she repeated, "What?"

Isaiah jerked his head toward the window, and she expressed an oh-my-something, then hopped to her knees to watch the rescue hopefully not unravel.

I stood behind her and got as close as I could, but really it was all shades of black out there, nothing truly discernible.

Minutes passed, maybe another hour, maybe not, and then the helicopter lights went out. We lost sight of everything, the black shades of sea and sky darkening to tar. Like the boat was drenched in a starless galaxy.

My phone chimed.

Bern and his sister looked at me with expectation, and Navy eyed me with annoyance.

"Everyone's safe," I reported. "Even the dog. Landed on the boat for now and heading back to the Coast Guard ship once we get out of the storm."

"Hallelujah," Isaiah breathed.

Navy nodded, and their eyes caught. It didn't bother me anymore, though.

I'd do the pit all over again, if it meant coming through knowing she wouldn't leave my side.

Day 5: Skagway

~~6:00 a.m. – 5:00 p.m.~~ 12:00 p.m. – 5:00 p.m.

Navy

The announcement woke me: "ATTENTION PASSENGERS: WE HAVE ARRIVED SAFELY IN SKAGWAY AND APOLOGIZE AGAIN FOR THE DELAY. INSTEAD OF THE ELEVEN HOURS SCHEDULED HERE, YOU NOW ONLY HAVE FIVE. WE WILL BE LEAVING PROMPTLY AT FIVE P.M. TO GET BACK ON SCHEDULE.

THANK YOU AGAIN FOR BEARING WITH US LAST NIGHT. WE APOLOGIZE FOR ANY INCONVENIENCE BUT KNOW YOU UNDERSTAND THAT OF UTMOST IMPORTANCE WAS COMING TO THE AID OF THOSE IN PERIL. ALL ARE SAFE, DRY, AND WELL.

ON A LIGHTER NOTE, WE ASK THAT YOU ENSURE YOUR VALUABLES ARE LOCKED IN THE PROVIDED SAFES IN YOUR

STATEROOM CLOSETS. REGRETTABLY, SOMETHING HAS GONE MISSING FROM A PASSENGER'S ROOM, AND ONCE AGAIN, WE ASK THAT IF YOU HAVE ANY INFORMATION, YOU WOULD COME TO PASSENGER SERVICES IMMEDIATELY."

Wait. Did that mean it was noon?

I shot up in bed and looked at the clock. Sure enough, I'd slept past eight. Unbelievable.

Wandering through our suite, I headed out to the common area and its balcony, then into Mom and Guy's side. No one was around. Back in my space, I noticed the note taped to the mirror: *Train ride at 2 p.m., Lovey. We'll meet you there. XO, Mom.*

I showered and got ready as fast as I could: jeans, tee-shirt, cardigan, boots. Make-up, earrings, maybe a light scarf.

As I grabbed the scarf off the pile on my chair, Isaiah's jewelry box fell to the floor.

I'd only looked at it that one morning before confronting him, and then barely when I'd shown it to the saleswoman. If I remembered correctly, it had been stunning. Under different circumstances, it would have been the perfect fit. Biting my bottom lip, I scooped it up, opened the box, and stared.

The way the gold wasn't flat, but wavy in the softest of ways, reminded me of the sea even without the sapphire chip. Not that I could put it on and give Isaiah the wrong idea, but could I keep it and wear it when he was gone? I'd buy it from him, but since he'd so far refused to take it back, insisting it was a gift, I doubted he'd let me give him money for it. Not that I wanted to find him and ask. I wanted to find Jesse. I wanted to spend the day with Jesse.

For now then, I'd put it in the safe like the announcements had instructed. I made my way into Mom and Guy's closet. Shoving all their clothes down the rod for easier access, I had to stand on my very tiptoes to punch in my birthday. No dice.

My mom's birthday.

My dad's death day. All normal passwords of hers.

Nothing.

When did she and Guy get engaged? About four months ago, on a Saturday. Maybe the 12th? No. The 14th? No. the 13th?

Yes! Bingo!

As I slotted the box next to my mom's travel case, my pinky caught on a loose chain, the pendant of which dropped out to pool in my palm.

Gold. Sapphire. Bezel set. Not in a box.

No.

No.

Stepping onto the carry-on suitcase Guy had stashed there, I peered in to find two wallets, a pile of what looked to be fifties, and a loose stash of casino chips stuffed in the far back.

My jaw dropped as it all clicked into place. *That's* why I'd recognized the lady in the pit. She'd been the one Guy talked to for so long when we were boarding. And he'd been in the bar to see Wally, had told my mom to warn me, so I could warn Jesse.

And he never stopped shopping for jewelry for my mom.

Was it all stolen? Everything he'd ever given her?

But when had he been in Ethel's room? Not that it was all that hard to believe, I guess, that he had been. They did go way back, and they were always at the art auctions together. Sometimes just the two of them even, when my mom was at Bingo with Liza. If he'd been waiting for her while she was finishing getting ready, was he that daring?

Or arrogant, maybe. He was definitely that arrogant.

How could he have sat at dinner and looked my mom in the face while everyone accused Wally?

The door opened behind me. His noise preceded him, a guttural *hmm* I'd heard out of him before when he was displeased. Turning around, the necklace still dangling from my hand and the safe open behind me, I swallowed hard.

I'd thought maybe I'd been in stare-downs before—plenty of girls at my various past schools were all about staring down the new girl so she didn't get any ideas—but he brought it to a whole new level.

"Navy Rose." The lilt of a threat was laced through his tone.

"Guy Southard?" But what I meant was, *is it really you who did this?*

"What do you have there?"

I looked at it, swallowed, swallowed again to try and lubricate my dry, unworking vocal cords, then squeaked, "A necklace?"

He closed the distance between us in two strides and snatched it out of my hand. Throwing it into the safe and slamming the door shut, he squeezed my arm and pushed me back, so quick and hard that I stumbled off the suitcase. He leaned in, breath on my face. Turning from whatever it was he'd had for lunch, it occurred to me I was cornered in a closet.

I had nowhere to go.

"You have nothing there, do you understand me?"

"My mom will never be okay with this," I said, hoping my tone was even and sure, though my stomach was scrambling up my throat in panic.

"Your mom," he snickered. "You try and get smart, I'll take her down with me."

Biting my tongue, I tried to think, tried to form coherent sentences, but the horror was too loud in my ears. Ringing. Alarms.

"Bye, bye, Mommy." He shoved me into the wall and backed up. "Locked in jail, behind bars. Little orphan Navy. Got it?"

I gulped. "Got it."

He spun and stormed out, slamming the door behind him and forgetting whatever it was he came back for. I sunk to the floor under his suit coats and felt for my phone with trembling hands.

SOSOSOSOSOSOS, I sent Jesse. *Meet me off the ramp.*

But then, as I sat there amidst the smell of Guy's clothes agitating softly around me, I realized it wasn't so easy.

I couldn't tell Jesse, couldn't ask him what to do, because I knew what he'd say. He'd say I had to turn him in, right away, no matter what. I would say that too. At least, I would have until it was my mom's head on the line. She was all I had. She was my only.

Jesse would be all about the truth and the right thing and helping Danilo out, but what if Guy *could* frame her? Could they send her to jail? What would I do then?

And how stupid to think of running to Jesse, who I'd only known for a few days. I should be running to my mom. That's what moms were for. But how do I tell a woman who's been searching my entire life for a man, that the pick she took so long to decide on was the wrong one?

Isaiah

Navy was rushing down the hall.

I tried to get her attention, but nothing registered until she ran into me.

Glancing up, she slumped over. Let her shoulders fold against me, dropped her face to my chest.

"Are you shaking?" I ran my hands up her arms and oh-good-Lord-into-her-hair on her shoulders. It was as silky and thick as it looked.

"How do you calm down, Isaiah, when you find out something you don't want to know?"

"When it's happened to me, I always went to brush out the horses." It was bad enough my dad was cheating on my mom, but being sworn to secrecy, as a kid, was terrifying. *You can never tell, Zay, okay? Or we can't come here anymore.* I never quite knew if it was the affair I wasn't supposed to tell about, or the fact that the affair was with a man.

By then, I'd already been obsessed with horses and tack and trail rides. The hunting came later, but the life had hooked me the same way it had my dad. So deep inside my belly that ripping it from me would've taken half of who I was with it.

"I don't have any horses," she whispered.

"I know." Flattening a palm on her back, I guided her to the big windows in the hall. There was enough of a ledge to sit there. Only sitting, it was awkward—creepy even—to keep my fingers in her mane.

Hands in my lap, I cleared my throat. "It was the motion. Reminding me to breathe with every stroke. The clatter of hooves, the soft neighs, the smell." I offered her my hand, palm up, in case she needed something to hold onto. She took it and looked at me. "You fill yourself with something else until you're used to it," I added. "Until you can live with it. Until you can understand it."

"Sort of like what Jesse's dad is doing?"

"I think he's just a drunk."

She shook her head, opened her mouth like she was going to defend him, bit her lip.

"Breathe," I suggested.

Nodding, she did. I did too, alongside her, slow at first, shaky. Then more regulated, deeper and calmer, until our chests were heaving a steady rise and fall. Until the air rushing out of our noses could be heard over the soft shuffle of a scattered crowd filing off the ship.

"There," I soothed. "That better?"

"What if I never get to a place where I can live with it?" She tossed the breathing exercise and turned to me, eyes dark and stormy. I'd never noticed that about them before. "What happens if I can never understand it?"

The affair had been easier to live with than the accident that killed them. Especially since the whispers at the funeral implied my dad had lost control on purpose. I guess when you're depressed, no one gives you the benefit of the doubt.

I knew better though. He would never have taken them both from me like that. Even so, it was when I'd learned that whispers have a burning, bitter sting.

There were far too many whispers still, back home. It was yet another reason I preferred the ranch.

"Sometimes you have to."

She shook her head, bit her lip.

"You fill yourself with something else until you can." *Fill yourself with me*, I wanted to say. *It can help us both*. "One day at a time, Navy. You only have to take it one day at a time." One moment, one brush, at a time.

Letting out a stiff, shaky breath, she let go of my hand and stood up. "Okay. Let's do this."

Jesse

We were done eating when I got Navy's text. My dad was still picking at his eggs, but only for my sake, because I'd been hounding him about food.

Slipping through the ship in no time, I spotted her as soon as I hit the ramp. Next to the silver rail at the bottom where the overhang stopped, she was picking at her nails.

Isaiah stood next to her, arms folded like a bodyguard. Had she called him first?

"What's up?" I asked. "Everything okay?"

Her gaze shot to Isaiah, like he knew. Like he was her confidante, and she didn't want to say, so she was hoping he might explain.

Or was he the emergency?

I put an arm around her and started walking her away from him, toward town. But she stopped short and looked up at me. Something must have happened, no doubt. Her eyes were different. Guarded.

Turning, I glared at Isaiah, trying to reconcile his mood with hers, but before I could figure anything, she asked him if he was coming.

She didn't wait for his answer, but slipped her hand inside

mine, clutched my fingers, and pulled me along the giant cement pier toward the sea, rather than toward town.

So it wasn't about him, and he might actually know something I didn't.

Then again, it was my hand she grabbed. We were solidly past the shudder of germ-induced thoughts and running for the nearest hand sanitizer. There was no more leaning away to keep me out of her personal space bubble. This was a feat in and of itself that I did not take lightly.

She let go once we got to the end of the pier. On the left, beyond a metal railing, rose a wall of rock that stretched up into a full-blown mountain. Ages-old graffiti marked the spot for decades of Marine platoons that had touched down here.

Navy laid her jacket on the railing, then hung herself over her jacket. Her head dropped low, hair dragging in the soft wind, and chunky wooden earrings brushing her cheeks.

"It would feel better to talk about it," I said. It was what my mom was always wanting and what my dad could never give her. Something I never thought would be difficult for me, but kind of understood now.

Because it was different when you were really hurting, and different when you kept taking the same hits. The deeper the wound went, the harder it was to look it in the face and voice it out loud.

"I know it might not feel that way," I choked out. "But it always feels better to get it out."

Isaiah watched the back of Navy's head as he picked at a chip in the railing with his fingernail, which was darkened at the edges like he could no longer wash all the hard work off of him.

Navy took a deep breath and straightened herself, calm now. Standing tall, she took a few steps and turned back to face us.

"I can't," she replied. "Not yet." She swallowed hard. "But I need you guys to stay with me, okay?" She looked back and forth between us. "Until I figure out what to do, you can't leave my side."

Navy

The train rumbled around us, trapping me with Guy on a moving box to nowhere.

It was dressed in faux oak paneling and chocolate brown seats, with big windows and a fair amount of legroom, and I was doing my damndest to pretend everything was the same as it was two hours ago.

At least I had Jesse and Isaiah flanking me. I needed them as buffer and to help me feel normal. Not that Guy would confront me in public, but how could he be laughing with the old ladies in the seat in front of them, after what happened in our stateroom? My insides were still shaking.

We sat on the other side of the aisle and three seats back.

Me by the window, then Jesse, then Isaiah. There was so much between us, but I still shivered from the proximity to Guy's cold, dead heart.

Full-time RVer, my ass. Full-time traveling thief was more like it. How did I get mom out of that without ruining her in the process?

Fill yourself with something else, that's what Isaiah suggested. And Jesse, the opposite: talk about it, hold it and feel it. If I told them what was actually happening, would one of them flip and agree with the other? Probably not.

Staring through the window, I zoned out to the blur of the scenery. Trees, streams rushing white over rocks, and mountains in the distance cutting a deep V around Skagway. The rattle of the seats, the rumble of the floor beneath my feet, the obnoxious clacking of the train on its track, and the slightly less obnoxious chatter of the tour guide, all of it helped numb my thoughts.

Until, of course, she tried to convince us we were taking a treacherous-looking train bridge that gapped a deep valley, which from here made me woozy, the height of it. When we flew over a newer, stronger version instead, Guy teased the guide about her sneaky ways. As if sneaky was something to write home about.

I thought I might be sick.

Climbing over Jesse and Isaiah, I rushed to the back of the train car and burst outside. It was a small space with a shallow overhang and a short iron rail to keep people from falling to their death. Not my idea of an oasis, but I needed the fresh air and distance from Guy.

Leaning back against the wall of the car, the farthest I could get from the drop to the blurred ground beneath us, I worked on breathing the same way Isaiah and I had earlier.

The door slid open and both Jesse and Isaiah looked around while stepping for the edge.

"Good call," Jesse said, pressing himself against the decorative rail.

I wanted to yell at him that he might fall but couldn't get anything out. A polar bear might as well have been sitting on my chest, and though we were going pretty fast, I think the fuzzy scenery had more to do with the tears in my eyes.

Isaiah stepped up next to Jesse and rested his hands on the metal, leaning back instead of forward at least. "This'll make you dizzy."

"You guys aren't helping," I managed.

Jesse glanced back at me, then to the drop a few feet next to us, where he could easily tumble down the side of a mountain. "Ah, right. Heights."

Isaiah took a few steps closer to the door, and Jesse moved next to me, pressing himself belly first against the wall. I meant to laugh—it began as a laugh, as relief—but tears came out instead. Choking on them, and not wanting either of them to see me cry, I covered my face with my hands.

"Hey." Jesse tried to pull my arms down, but I wouldn't let him, so he drew himself against me, a loose hug. The wind whooshed past, the train clacked on, and our bodies shook against each other.

I couldn't do this. I couldn't take it one day at a time, and I couldn't live with it.

Even if the truth ruined her, I had to tell my mom. It was that or destroy both of us by living a lie. She was a mother. She'd know what to do, and she would take the lead.

She had to, because I had no idea where to start.

Isaiah

After the train ride, Delilah told Navy she needed to freshen up for dinner. Navy told us we were coming with.

As Delilah and Guy disappeared into their stateroom, Navy took a deep breath. "I need to talk to my mom. I don't know if Guy will leave her, but I want you guys to wait in the hall." Chewing on her lip, she looked between us. "Is that okay? Will you sit in the hall for me?"

"Of course," Jesse said.

Sure, I nodded. Whatever. I'd sat in worse.

"Pretend you're waiting for me, and if Guy leaves, knock." Glancing to me, she added, "Or text me."

"How will you not know?" I asked. "It's one room."

"We have two, and a living area. Doors between."

"Fancy," Jesse teased.

She gave him a look, exasperated but intimate.

After waiting for another round of nods, she marched down to the next door, pointed at the floor in front of it, and slipped into her room.

"Do you think she's okay?" Jesse asked. "Does she seem different to you?"

"Yeah. And yeah."

"But if she seems different to both of us, and we've only known her as long as we have, then something bad must have happened."

"She's a survivor," I said, before I thought much about it. But she was, and this was what I didn't understand. "Navy and me? We're survivors."

Jesse eyed me through his curls. Not as viciously as I might've if someone had said that to me. "You think I'm soft, Isaiah?"

"Nothing wrong with it," I said, studying Navy's room number. "I wish I could be. Wish I still was."

He snorted. "That's irony right there."

"Irony how?"

"If you're really tough, you wouldn't be pouting about having to be."

I clenched my teeth. I wasn't pouting. I was relaying fact. Leaning back against the wall, I adjusted my cowboy hat so I didn't have to look at him.

After a few minutes, he muttered, "I wish she felt like she could talk to me."

My turn to snort. "She's known you for how many days?"

Didn't have to peek out from under my hat to feel his squirm and squiggle. Yeah, he wanted to think they were tight, but reality shed a whole different light.

Except, I felt like I'd kicked a puppy. Rolling my eyes, I added, "She didn't talk to me, either."

Guy and Delilah's door opened, and we both snapped to attention.

They stared at us, and we stared at them.

Delilah's gaze settled on Jesse, and she clutched her purse tighter. Guy shifted like there was a burr under his saddle.

Had Ethel told him Jesse was one of the two original suspects?

Of course she had. She'd told everyone who'd listen, then Gram told everyone who'd listen, then Delilah told everyone who'd listen. It was a miracle the whole ship wasn't grabbing their purses tighter when he walked by.

"Delilah, love, I don't want Navy hanging out with a suspect."

Handing her purse to Guy, perhaps so she wouldn't have to walk it past Jesse, Delilah rapped on Navy's door.

Navy yanked it open, nearly breathless. Peeking out, she saw Guy and forcibly relaxed her pose. "What's up?"

"Jesse's a suspect," her mom whispered, as if he might not

be able to hear. "It was one thing before you knew, but now . . ."

"I knew before you did, Mom. I knew before Ethel told you this morning, and I knew before you texted me."

"Baby, what if he's casing our room right now?" she whispered.

"He's sitting there because I asked him to," Navy snapped.

"Honey, I really think—"

"He's innocent, Mom."

"Don't be so sure," Guy said. Crossing a leg, he leaned against the wall and tucked Delilah's purse under his arm. "Everyone here is a stranger."

Navy choked out an unintelligible response. Like a horse rearing and bucking in her throat. Then she slammed the door.

Jesse

Guy usually set the tone at dinner, but tonight he was distracted, maybe by me, now that I was *the suspect.*

Delilah and Ethel were cooing at Guy from either side, as if trying to soothe a disgruntled rock star, and Navy was silent.

Until she was ready to talk, all I could do was distract her, make her feel better like she'd been doing this whole trip for me. I wanted to grab her hand under the table, but I was on her right side and she was eating, so there was nothing but thigh to squeeze. I'd had her in my arms a few times, and she'd been holding my hand almost the entire day, but a thigh seemed a bit much.

"What's everyone up to tonight?" I asked, trying to diffuse the tension another way.

Only, that seemed to make it more awkward.

Yeah, they'd had an entire day to buzz about it. Who cared that I'd been cleared or that their trusted children were my alibi. Judgments and prejudice ran deeper than common sense and logic.

"Liza and I are going to the show," Delilah replied, when no one else did. She might be willing to publicly doubt the Kowalski character, but she wouldn't let a polite question go unanswered.

"Just you two?" Navy asked, her voice hoarse. And as she cleared it, without even a thought, my palm reached for her leg.

"Do you want to come?" her mom asked.

Navy looked from Liza to her mom and back again, then shook her head. "No."

"I'm going to hit the art auction one last time," Guy said.

"I'll go with you." Ethel smiled. "I have my eye on that one in the gallery, but I'd rather not pay full price for it. Hopefully they'll bring it up tonight."

Navy's palm slid over my hand, but she didn't push it away. Instead she held on like she was drowning. "When's the show start?" she asked her mom, tone tight like her grip.

"We'll head over right after dinner." Delilah flashed her an absent smile. "What are you guys doing?"

"Toni asked me to help DJ." One tip for smooth song transition delivered to the coordinator they had DJing the dance party, and Toni decided I needed to teach them everything I knew.

"Dessert for anyone?" Balasz asked, swooping in silently as usual.

"I can't decide," I said, tilting my head back at him. "What do you suggest?"

Navy let out a little groan, and she was right. I should know better than to tell him I couldn't decide. As soon as the words were out, I regretted them.

"I shall bring all for you, Mr. Jesse." He put a hand up as I opened my mouth to object. We'd played this dance many times already this week, and he always won. "You share what you don't eat."

With a sigh, I turned back to the table.

Navy leaned toward me. "I think I've gained five pounds already, the way he feeds us."

Rubbing my belly with my free hand, I agreed, "Why don't I learn?"

"Because you like picking off three desserts?"

"Okay, but after the soup and salad I can't decide on, and the two entrees I'm waffling between, three desserts really seems like overkill."

A grin spread across her face and she sighed, as if all she needed was this little bit of normal. Honestly, I'd eat eighteen desserts if it would pull a smile like that, and from a girl I'd known less than a week.

For the second time that day, I got a glimpse of understanding. Of what it might feel like if I'd known her twenty years, and she was leaving me.

Navy

My palms were still sweating from dinner.

I wiped them off once again on my jeans, back and forth and back and forth, the same motion that Toni was using on Jesse's shoulders. He'd only been DJing an hour so far, he didn't need a back massage. Plus, working an iPod hooked up to a sound system didn't seem all that stressful to me. And I thought this was for the coordinators to learn something, not just her, but she was his only groupie. The others were dancing in the crowd.

"Look." Bern elbowed me. "I think I found the swan."

He had his phone and its constellation app up in the window. We were in a dark corner and his screen highlighted what looked like a stick person with no legs, hands up in frustration.

"That's ridiculous. How is that a swan?"

"Hey, it's better than Hercules."

Which was a very good point. Hercules had almost looked like a swastika.

Toni leaned over Jesse's shoulder to see what song he was choosing next. Shouldn't she be coordinating the whole group, instead of figuratively holding his hand?

I wanted to be holding his hand. I wanted to be telling him all the things I couldn't tell him. What if I walked over to that stupid DJ table and pulled Jesse away, right from under Toni's nose. *Come with me,* I'd say. *I need to talk to you.*

And then I would tell him about Guy and he would say, *turn him in; free Danilo.* Of course he would. This I knew and it was only day five. It's what I would have said too, but look how quickly they snagged Jesse when he was innocent. How easy for that same thing to happen to my mom, but easier, because this time they'd have proof.

I couldn't be as good as him in this situation. It would ruin everything that wasn't already ruined.

"Scorpio?" Bern asked, while shaking the screen as if that would make the shape more clear.

"Barely," I agreed, flipping my phone over and over in my palm, a one-handed maneuver. "If you have an overactive imagination."

"Navy, you're supposed to be playing along here. What gives?"

I mean, really, if I were Guy, I wouldn't take my mom down with me, I'd blame the kid. My finger *had* touched down on that necklace, he'd seen it. He knew my prints were on stolen goods. The casino chips probably had too many to read, and the purse? For all I knew, he could've worn a glove, or wiped everything clean. I didn't know anything about fingerprint science, but I'd feel better if I had concrete proof that it was him before gambling that my mom and I would come out of it, unscathed.

Being his almost-wife, it's possible my mom would have some idea where to find that proof. Maybe she already knew something that she didn't know she knew.

Letting my cell fall screen side up, I woke it and texted her: *I need urgent kissing advice. Can we talk at intermission?*

Bern peered down at it. "You are wasting a wealth of knowledge, sitting right here next to you. You do not need your mom."

Except, I wasn't going to tell him that's not really why I needed to talk to her.

"Pick Isaiah," he said. "For one week on a cruise ship, you pick the hot one, not the funny one. Funny ones are long term."

Toni's fingertips were still on Jesse, touching down on his shoulder as she whispered at him.

"Jesse is both," I noted. "Clearly I'm not the only one who thinks so."

"Meh." Bern went back to his screen. "Look at this conglomeration of random nothingness. Ophiuchus?" Shaking his head, he dropped his cell and turned to watch the five people dancing in front of us. "Fine. You're right. Star-gazing is hopeless."

With a soft ping, my phone lit up: *No intermission dear. After the show okay?*

Meet at the café? I replied. Could I actually get her out from under Guy's nose for five minutes? *It's super super important.* If nothing else, I needed to give her a head's up. Explain that it wasn't me, no matter what he might end up saying. We were smart women. We would figure something out.

"That dude could be an eagle," Bern said, bringing his constellation app up on the dancers instead of the window. It tried to follow and capture the few streams of light roiling from the disco ball, then locked up.

I need to get out of these heels, let's just do it in our room. I promised Guy I'd come straight back.

Of course she did. My fingers hovered over a possible *Guy or me? Pick.* But I couldn't quite go there. Not yet. Not in case he might see it.

Isaiah

Navy asked me to go to the teen lounge with them, but I was over it. I took one step in, and one step out. No. Priority was plan C. Figuring one out, anyway.

I needed somewhere I could think. After trying the outer deck, maneuvering around couples holding hands, I headed for Aunt Ethel's room. It would feel the most private and remote, but only without her in it. Good thing she was at the auction.

I needed peace and quiet. To focus and regroup.

Sliding my spare key through the slot, I yanked the door open with a whinny. Except it hadn't come from me. Then silence. I moved toward the armchair, froze in front of the little glass coffee table.

She wasn't at the auction.

She was here.

In bed, half covered by a naked man.

Oh, *shit*.

"Isaiah!" She grabbed a coffee mug from the nightstand and tossed it at me. "Get out!"

I ducked the projectile but could not look away.

Bare-assed in front of me like the mule he was, giving it to my aunt, was Guy fucking Southard. And between us, on the floor by my foot, was his wallet.

Quick thinking, from years of dealing with green-broke horses, I kicked it hard, under the bed as I turned to leave. Hopefully it made it to a corner he wouldn't be able to find.

Double-checking that the door was closed behind me, and I was safely in the hall, I pressed my back against the wall.

Holy horse shit. Was this what Navy was so upset about? Did her mom not know? Delilah had seemed totally fine at dinner. So Navy didn't know how to tell her, or maybe Delilah wouldn't believe her. Same as my mom never believed me.

But he's happy there, Mom, honest. Why don't we move to Montana?

I mean, now I could see, of course.

Racing back up the many flights of stairs—*I had proof for her*—I almost tripped on the final landing.

I was the hero now. I would be the hero.

Marching through the door, noise be damned, I searched the room and found only Bern and Jesse. Bern saw me and headed my way. We met in front of the DJ table. I panted out her name: "Navy?"

"Went to bed."

"I need to talk to her."

Bern tilted his head. "She wanted to talk to her mom first."

"What do you mean *first?* She doesn't know what—"

"I mean that's all she wants right now. Don't interrupt her."

"She tell you what's going on?"

"What's going on?" Jesse asked.

Bern glanced between us. "You two are idiots." His gaze settled on me. "She didn't have to tell me."

"Then you don't know what I'm talking about."

"What are you talking about?" Jesse asked, voice a little higher now, alarmed.

"Trust me, Cowboy. I saw her texts. Don't interrupt." Bern narrowed his eyes at Jesse. "You either."

Did that mean *Bern* knew? She told *Bern?*

Had I walked in earlier, would she have told me?

Except no. I'd screwed this up so many times over, there was no way. No hope. Until now, because I had proof. Proof that she was no doubt looking for. Proof that would help her.

And proof that might help me too. A solid plan C.

Day 6: At sea

Isaiah

I texted Navy first thing in the morning: *You up?*

It was early, seven. Guy's wrinkly ass and my aunt in heat was still branded into my brain. This meant I was up with the dawn, waiting to make shit happen. For Navy, and for me too.

Yes. Hiding in the teen lounge until Guy leaves for his spa appointment. Did you know they have muffins every a.m.?

Didn't know. On my way.

I jogged from our room to the elevator, tapped my boot on the shiny tile while the lift did the work for me, and hoofed it from the elevator into the lounge. Navy was curled up by the glass wall, muffin on a napkin, napkin on her knees.

"Want some?" she asked, as I sat down on the bench next to her.

I shook my head. "Not sure I'll ever be able to eat again."

"That's dramatic for a cowboy."

Glancing around, I checked that we were alone. "I know why you were upset."

She pinched off a blueberry. "You do?"

"I can prove it. I have proof for you, for your mom."

"What are you talking about?"

"You want to expose Guy. I want back on the ranch."

"You know about Guy?" She leaned toward me and the muffin tumbled to the floor. "What proof?"

"His wallet. He left it in my aunt's room."

"Holy shit. It places him there." Clasping my biceps, she tried to shake me. "You really think that will be enough? What about the others?"

"Who cares if there were others, your mom only needs to know there was one, right?"

Navy cocked her head and leaned back, letting go of me. "My mom?"

"Yeah, your mom."

"Isaiah, what are you talking about?"

"What are *you* talking about?"

"No, you first."

"Guy and Ethel?" I offered.

"Guy and Ethel what?"

"You know." I searched my brain for the most polite way to say it. "Mating. Breeding."

"Excuse me?"

Okay, so horse terminology didn't always save the day. "You weren't upset because you found out Guy and Ethel were having an affair?"

"No! I was upset because . . . *what?*"

"I saw it myself."

She blinked at me. And again.

"I'll go back sometime today, make sure the wallet's still there. Then, if your mom doesn't believe you, you can bring her over to see it."

She clasped a hand to her mouth and shook her head, kept shaking it. Like this was news. Like it was shocking.

"Wait," I said. "That's *not* why you were upset?"

"You think he's having sex with all these old women he flirts with?" She let out a horrible noise. "I might throw up."

"I think he's giving it to my aunt for now. That's all that matters."

She folded over, muffin tumbling to the floor. There was no Jesse here to hold her, but I didn't know if she'd let me, so instead I put a weak hand to her back, ran it tentatively up and down. Her hair slid against my bare skin and connected all sorts of dots, lighting up all sorts of pathways inside my brain.

"This is good," I pointed out. "Now you have proof."

"*How* is this good? All I see is it getting worse at every turn."

"What else were you upset about, if not that? Me and Jesse?"

"Ugh," she groaned. "Are you so self-absorbed that you think I'd be mooning around after two boys I met five days ago?"

I slouched. Put on my best apologetic face. "No?"

"I have to tell you something. Can I tell you something?"

"Of course Navy. I'm on your side."

"It's not good." She sniffled, biting down on her lip. "But you might be my only hope."

Navy

I held my breath when I finished, expecting Isaiah to sound the alarms, or for Guy to clasp my ankle and drag me away with him.

Instead, he laughed. "No way."

I exhaled, shaky and uncertain, even though Isaiah had the proof I needed, something that placed Guy, and only Guy, inside Ethel's room.

"All this time he acts like a total prick to Jesse and his dad, and it's really him?" He laughed again, a big booming *Ha.* Shaking his head, he added, "What a perfect bastard."

"So will you go to Benoît for me? If I have anything to do with it, if Guy thinks I was anywhere near turning him in, probably if he even knew we were having this conversation, I'd be toast."

"Of course. It's the ideal trade."

"Thank you." I stood. "I need to give my mom a heads up." How I was going to tell her that her fiancé was not only a thief but also a total skeezeball, I didn't know, but it had to be done. And this spa appointment might be my only chance.

"Wait."

I turned back to him.

"The trade?" he prodded.

Yeah, I'd been trying not to hear that. But how bad could it be? I could coo over a guy as well as my mom could. I just chose not to. "Fine. You help me, I'll help you."

"You help me first," he said. "Then I'll help you."

I stared at him.

"I won't do any of it until my grandma says I can go back to the ranch."

My mouth dropped open. What an asshole. Who was the trustworthy one here anyway? Wasn't he the one more likely to use me and walk away? On second thought, maybe I should be wondering if there even was a wallet. I wouldn't put it past him to use it as a bargaining chip, even if it didn't exist. I let out a short laugh of disbelief. Not that I should be surprised.

He looked up, a clear plea, "I need that ranch as bad as you need away from Guy, okay?"

"The situations are not comparable," I clipped, hand to my hip.

He crossed his arms. "That's the deal."

"What if it takes the rest of the trip, Isaiah? That doesn't help me!"

"Then do something obvious, like kiss me at dinner."

Kiss him at dinner? Was he out of his mind? I couldn't make out with someone I *wanted* at a dinner table, let alone kiss someone I didn't.

"Problem?" he challenged.

I dropped back to the seat with a frustrated growl. "I can't have you be my first kiss."

"Your first kiss?" He squinted at a me a little.

"I don't want to talk about it, I'm just saying I can't. I won't."

"I'm so disgusting you can't imagine kissing me?" He frowned, and his jaw twitched.

I rolled my eyes. "I've thought about it, of course, but after everything that's happened. After Jesse and I . . ."

He turned back to me and threw up a hand. "Perfect. Go find Jesse, get your first kiss over with, then come find me, and we'll make this happen."

"You don't get it. It's my first kiss. I'm not going to just *get it over with*"—I air-quoted with my fingers –"and I'm not going to make it happen. I want . . ." But I wasn't going to tell him what or how I wanted anything. Isaiah was too far gone to understand any of it.

"*You* don't get it," Isaiah said. "You want my help? My solution? Then you make it happen, one way or the other." He stood up, smashing my muffin in the process and smearing the blueberries on the floor. "You don't think you have any other option? Well, I don't either. So that's the deal. When you're ready, put on the necklace and I'll know."

He walked out, trailing crumbs as he went, and I didn't bother to tell him his boot was caked in delicious. I was too numb, like the cold sea outside and the wind howling against the window.

Or maybe not so numb, since water was dripping from my face. Okay, so I'd give myself a little bit to cry it out, to plan. And I'd clean up the mess Isaiah had left on the floor.

I didn't think I could let him stick his tongue in my mouth, no matter what the stakes. Germs, personal space, lack of character, and the recently discovered warped heart, it was all working against him.

I scrubbed the floor with my napkin until I was cleaning only what was already clean. That's how low I'd sunk, that I was scrubbing the dirty-nasty floor. Of course, at this very low point of my life, Toni walked in.

She stopped in front of me. "You okay, kid?"

Kid? She didn't seem to think Jesse was much of a kid, and he was only one year older than me. I stood and walked out, away from her and the remnants of Isaiah's deal that were haunting the room.

Down the stairs. There were a lot of them. Too many. But my brain had too many thoughts, it had found out too many things. I needed to get a hold of myself.

Two more days. Three if you counted the early morning we were landing and getting off the boat. I had to give my mom some time, right? To get used to it, before Isaiah turned Guy in.

So she knew too, in case I couldn't effectively satisfy my end of the deal. I mean, no matter what, worst case scenario, she could still leave him—*we* could still leave him—and better to part ways on Saturday than after the move.

Yes, I had to tell her.

Mom? I texted. *Where are you?*

In the room.

I checked the time. Exactly on the hour, when Guy's appointment supposedly started. If he even had an appointment at all. Maybe he was with Ethel, looking for his wallet. What if when Isaiah checked back, the wallet was gone? Then what? Then even if I followed through my end of the bargain, what help could he be?

Ugh. Too many variables.

But that decided things. I had to talk to my mom. Maybe she could bust into Ethel's room right now, distract them, throw a fit. Maybe it could all work out another way. Without Isaiah. Without a fake kiss.

Alone? I double checked.

Yep.

Well, finally. I guess it was about time one thing went my way. I hurried down the rest of the stairs and flew into the hall. Opening my door, I locked it with the chain, then went around to her door and locked that one with the chain too. There could be no interruptions.

She was sitting on the couch in front of the sliding door that led to the balcony, feet propped up on the coffee table, flipping through a magazine and sipping tea. She watched as I took the armchair directly across from her and rested my elbows on my knees.

With a grin, she swung her feet off the table to mirror my posture. "Were you kissed?" she asked.

Opening my mouth wide, I drew in some air and replied on an exhale. "No."

She leaned back and crossed a leg. "Then what's up?"

Oh, Lord. How to ease into this? "Are you so sure about Guy?"

"Of course, honey. Why would you ask that?"

Maybe I could convince her to leave him *without* breaking her heart. "Well, aren't you sick of being a gypsy?"

"What's wrong with seeing the world and experiencing new things? Anyway, Ethel's more of a gypsy than us. Well, maybe free spirit is the better word. Liza says she sleeps around on these cruises, bless her heart."

I choked.

"You okay, dear?"

"I think you told me that already. I didn't believe it." Maybe there was more to this gossip than I gave her credit for. Dropping my head forward, I tried to regroup.

"Baby, what's going on?" She reached out and settled her fingertips on my wrist.

"What if I told you that Guy was the thief?"

Her face went slack, and her hand dropped from mine. "I'd say maybe you're old enough to know the truth."

"What truth? What are you talking about?"

"Why do you think we move all the time?"

I sat up straighter in my chair. We moved because she couldn't settle, because she was chasing my dad away, or running from him.

I shook it out of my head, the ridiculousness of what she was implying. She must be protecting Guy.

"No. Don't do this. You don't want this, Mom. This life? What about Daddy? What would Daddy think?"

Scooting forward on her seat, she took my hands with a sigh. "There's so much to cover there. Let me start with the theft."

"Don't even try to tell me it was you, just so I won't turn him in. Lie to yourself all you want, Mom, but don't start lying to me." Plus, *he* was the one in Ethel's room. Oh God, did she know about that too?

"No, no, honey. It was him. But see, that's the thing. When he asked me to marry him, he said he'd steal *for* me from now on, so I didn't have to put myself at risk. Like, I could be a stay-at-home mom finally, like I've always wanted. See? He's perfect for us."

"He's not. He's . . ."

"He's not your daddy, I know."

I wrenched my hands from hers and wrapped them

together against my chest. "You've been *stealing* all these years? What about the money Daddy left you?"

"There was no inheritance." She put on a long face and took her time coloring it in with sympathy. "That's just what I told you."

The pieces clicked into place. The conversation. Her words. She looked sad and honest, not one bit of mask in place that she wore for everyone else. This was the face I remembered from when I was young, and it set me off-balance. I put a hand up to stop it. To stop everything. To hold on.

"I thought we kept moving because you were trying to find someone to love the way you loved Daddy. I thought you weren't so Christian anymore because it hurt to remember him. I thought—" Breathe. Deep, full breaths.

"Listen, none of that matters. What matters is you're not going to turn anyone in."

"None of that matters? Daddy doesn't matter?"

Her expression went stern. Something I hadn't seen since I was eight and was in her purse for gum without asking. "Your dad wasn't a pastor. I told you that because God knew my moral compass wasn't big enough for the both of us. Now stop sniveling and tell me you're not going to ruin our future over something so minor. It's not like he *murdered* someone."

"Dad wasn't a pastor?"

She flashed her right hand. "Why do you think I keep all these rings? One of them is from your father. I was juggling too many and it backfired." She pointed to the solitaire on her middle finger, "He was in the navy." To the small diamond chips shaped into a magnolia, "He had navy blue eyes." And to the three rocks lined up in a row on her ring finger, "He had a yacht on the sea."

With a ping, everything I ever was or thought myself to be shattered and crumbled into my gut, leaving me with nothing to stand on, nothing to frame my life inside. All the good I thought I'd come from, the pastor and the love and the family and the life we'd left behind. All the things I held onto, none of it had been real. Did that mean none of me was real?

I hunched over, certain I was going to be sick.

She stood and came to rub my back. I didn't have the energy to fight her.

"The important thing is, Baby, this is your family. Now you know."

"He said he'd take you down with him."

"Of course he did, hon. He was trying to protect me. So you wouldn't know what you clearly can't handle hearing. Romantic, if you think about it."

"Is it romantic that he's screwing Ethel?" I asked.

"Well, not romantic, exactly, but . . ."

"You knew that too?" I stood, and her hand dropped from where it had been on my back to grip the chair.

"Listen, Guy has a ton of money, he just steals for fun. And Ethel?" She waved her hand. "He's marrying me, and he makes me happy." Her expression drew tighter as if maybe she didn't believe everything she was saying. "This is the way it is, and this is the way it stays. I've been a great mom, and I will continue to be. Don't ruin my life like I've been careful, thus far, not to ruin yours." Grabbing my chin, she twisted it up so I had no choice but to look at her. Steady, severe, and stern, she commanded, "Say it. Say you won't tell."

But I couldn't speak. Jerking away, I ran to my bathroom, slammed the door, and threw up in the toilet.

Jesse

I couldn't find Navy anywhere, and I couldn't find Isaiah either. At sea all day, confined to this boat, and I felt like we'd lost a week.

Were they together? Was it because Toni had been all over me last night? Navy had to know it meant nothing. She had to have seen me watching her whenever she turned, and she had to know I didn't want Toni all over me like that. I'd only allowed it because I was trying to get information on Danilo, trying to find his way out, trying to get her to *do* something, and trying to convince her there was even something to do.

But maybe Navy was mad regardless. Or Isaiah found her even though Bern had told us to leave her alone. Could something he said have changed things?

I'd even resorted to texting, and now was hoping to corner

her in her room. She had to be there, getting ready for the formal dinner, and I had to talk to her before we got to the table. I wouldn't let tonight be another night that wasn't about us. If she wanted me alone again, all she had to do was say it.

Standing in front of her stateroom, I rested my forehead on the wall to compose myself from the day's search and panic mode. Once ready, I rapped lightly on the door.

"Who is it?" she asked weakly.

"Jesse. Can we talk?"

The door swung open and she muttered, "You too?"

"Me too what?"

"You have something big to tell me too?"

"Who else had something big to tell you?" I followed her into her room and closed the door. Her phone, a deck of cards, and a near-empty bag of gummy cherries were on the floor near her closet, like she'd just emerged from a den beneath her clothes.

"It doesn't matter." Looking up at the ceiling, she exhaled an unsteady breath. "I can't talk about it now." Spinning, she moved into the room and sat on a chair by a little glass table at the foot of her bed. She had two twins and a door leading out opposite the one I'd come in.

I moved to open the door and check out what was behind it, but she caught my sleeve.

"Don't open that."

Something more had happened today, I could tell by the

way she was drooping—her shoulders, her waist, her knees even, and of course her head. I might not have known her very long, but she'd never seemed the drooping type. She was all class, tall and proud and unflinching.

Sitting on the bed in front of her, I noticed her face was blotchy. "Are those hives? Are you okay?"

She opened her mouth, then closed it.

"Is this about me?" I whispered. "Last night, Toni and I—"

"It's not you," she interrupted with a shake of her head. "You're the only good thing about my life right now."

"What happened, Navy?"

"Please don't call me that."

"Don't call you Navy?"

"Call me Midnight."

"Did Isaiah do this?"

She didn't answer right away, but then, "No, actually, he's a selfish asshole, but that's the least of my worries."

I offered her my hand, and she slid hers into it. "Wanna talk about it?" I asked.

"No. I need to rally for dinner." She pulled away from me and rubbed under her eyes. "Can you tell I've been crying?"

I shook my head. I mean, aside from the blotchy hives.

"Stay here while I get ready?"

I nodded. She went to the bathroom and closed the door behind her, while I took the chair she'd been sitting in and tried not to stare at the bra peeking out of the pile of clothes on her spare bed.

When the water stopped, I closed my eyes, and when the door clicked open, I squeezed them tighter. The closets were exposed to the hall, and there was no room to put on an evening gown in the teeny tiny bathroom.

The rustle of fancy dress fabric had me drawing up an image in my head, no matter how hard I tried to think of tattoo ink and the feel of the needle. Then I heard her move back to the bathroom and start up a hair dryer. Phew. That was better.

Next thing I knew, I'd nodded off, and she was tapping my knee. Her hair was dry and wavy, makeup dark and dramatic, and her lips a deep red, three shades darker than her dress.

She smiled, like nothing had happened, like she hadn't had hives from crying an hour before or asked me to call her by another name. "You fell asleep," she said.

"Yeah, I went to this crazy club last night. The DJ was bangin'."

She laughed and reached for my hand. "Tonight, after dinner, can it just be us?"

Isaiah

My nicest plaid cowboy shirt looked a little odd with the black dress pants and shiny business shoes we'd picked up in Juneau, but they let me in this time.

"It's because you left the hat," Gram said, brushing my

cowlick back with a spit-shined finger. I swatted her hand away. I wasn't seven.

Jesse sat next to Navy, the necklace still not around her neck.

Slamming into my chair, I glared at her, trying to will it onto her neck with the pure force of my mind. She ignored me, though. Like she was bombproof. And I was breathing like a sour horse.

"I can't believe they haven't made an announcement yet," Guy was saying. "When was the last one?"

"Yesterday, right Ethel?" Delilah asked. "Because of your money?"

Guy checked his fancy watch. "I reported my wallet stolen twelve hours ago."

I tried to catch Navy's eye, but she wouldn't have it.

"It must have happened at breakfast," Delilah said.

"You eat breakfast in the room every morning," Navy pointed out.

Her mom shot her a look. It wasn't very motherly. "Not this morning, dear. This morning we went to the buffet."

"I can't believe they haven't caught him yet," I said, careful to make my tone clear and unconcerned. "Gonna take a witness, I guess."

That got Navy's attention on me, viciously. But she had a choice to make, and we were running out of time.

Navy

Stupid Isaiah, dropping hints all through dinner. He was going to get me in more trouble with Guy, and my own mother, if he didn't shut up. How could they not already be suspicious, the way he was muttering and carrying on, thinking he sounded all innocent?

If he wanted to get me used to the idea of making his grandma think we were together, he should be working on making me like him more, not less.

The question was, would I ever be okay with this life my mom seemed to want? I mean, she was my mom, the only person who'd always been there for me, and she wanted me to drop it. She'd begged me. Threatened me. But after the way I'd been raised, though the irony there was overwhelming, was it even possible for me to look away?

If I did, then this was my life too, at least for another few years. And if something fell down on Guy later, I couldn't be sure he wouldn't blame me, the easy scapegoat. That could happen at any time, if I didn't take my chance and turn him in now.

On the other hand, if I did turn him in, everything went back to how it was, which didn't sound so great either, now that I knew my own mother had been moving us to stay ahead of suspicion. But she would never frame me; she would take the fall if it came down to it.

Right?

I mean, unless maybe I ripped her meal ticket out from under her.

Whereas, if I let her keep Guy, then I'd have the promise of at least two years in the same place. I could make a friend, maybe even keep one.

Did that make me a party to it all, now that I knew? Was I a thief because I went along with it? Daddy would roll in his—

I choked on my mashed potatoes, covering my mouth with a napkin as I coughed. Jesse, alarmed, rubbed my back. My mom rushed to do the same from the other side. She was acting like nothing had happened. Though I guess none of it was news to her. But how could she act like nothing had changed *for me*? It was her fault, for letting me believe in a dad who didn't exist. Had she raised me without a moral compass, then this decision wouldn't be so hard.

I would keep her out of it, of course. She was my mother and all I had. It was Guy anyway, technically, and he could try to take her down with him, but we had proof he was in Ethel's room and she wasn't. Plus, she'd said this was the deal. That he was doing all the lifting for her, so her fingerprints shouldn't be on any of it. And they were engaged, so maybe that was like being married and she wouldn't have to testify. Or maybe that was only true in the movies.

Good thing the tears in my eyes were explained away with the choking. Jesse was squeezing my shoulder and Isaiah prodding me with his gaze: *Do it, do it, do it, do it.*

Selfish prick.

He was in a rescue boat right now, no matter what he thought, compared to my sinking ship.

"Wanna get out of here?" Jesse asked.

I blinked over at him. "You'd forgo your desserts for me?"

One side of his mouth drew up in a half smile. "Any day."

I nodded, and he scooted his chair back before helping me out of mine. Without a word in response to my mom and Isaiah calling out for us, we walked briskly away.

Thank God for Jesse's dad, who didn't say much. Because when he did—like right now, to help us escape—it shut the table down.

"Surprised you didn't strip search my son, Guy, for that wallet of yours."

Jesse

"There's supposed to be some whale-watching tonight," I said, slipping my hand through Navy's as we hit the elevators. When she didn't say anything, I added, "The naturalist is going to be on the speakers, helping us look. Where should we watch from?"

The elevator doors opened and we slid inside. She hit all the buttons.

"I was thinking the teen lounge would be okay," I said.

Squinting to read her, I found no agreement in her expression. "Maybe the Sunrise Court? Or the piano lounge." Nothing. Dead air. Dead face.

Finally she said, "Somewhere no one can find us."

I swallowed. "You want to be alone?"

"I don't want anyone to find us. I don't want to see my mom, Guy, or Isaiah. I don't want to talk to them, or listen to them, or breathe the same air as them."

Something had definitely gone down.

"My room?" I asked, but it was muffled in cotton balls and disbelief. My dad had by now adapted to the time change, so he wouldn't be rolling in until the alcohol bottles were empty, and a stateroom was the most private place on the ship.

As the elevator dinged open on the twelfth deck, she stepped out. I'd forgotten that her hand was in mine, that's how right it felt, and as I stood there, wondering what was on the twelfth deck, the slack in our arms met its limit and I was yanked along after her.

She hit the stairs so fast in her heels I worried she'd trip, down down down to level eight. "I'm changing, then your room," she said to my confused face.

Leading me in, she sat me again in the chair at the foot of her bed, the one that faced the mirror on the wall, the wall that separated her room from her closet. The closet that had no door, where I could hear her gown swishing to the ground.

Emerging in her uniform—skinny jeans and white tee—

plus a dark baggy sweatshirt, she twisted her hair into a messy bun on top of her head. Not bothering to change her earrings from the sparkly stone studs that matched her evening gown, she slipped her feet into flip-flops and held a hand out for me.

My insides locked up with the anticipation of her skin against mine, and more than just her hand, like when we'd danced or when we'd sat in the hall the other night. I wanted to do all those things again, one million times each, and we only had two days left.

She wiggled her fingers. "You okay?"

I stood, and in three long strides our fingers jolted together. "Never better."

Navy

My life had fissured and was crumbling around me. Or maybe it was me who'd fissured—some of me splintering off, holding onto Jesse and the illusion of who I'd been, while other bits shook from the foundation to move in another direction. Only I didn't know which direction that would be yet.

It did occur to me that I could tell him everything and ask for advice. Only, I couldn't bear for him to see me the way I now saw myself. Not yet. I needed some space from it. From them and it, and here in Jesse's room maybe I could savor that for a few hours before I had to make a decision.

"Do you want to talk?" he asked, emerging from the closet

while pulling a shirt on over his bare chest.

But I couldn't look away from his stomach, the wiry muscles and how low his shorts hung, the cut of his hips . . . he really wasn't as skinny as he seemed.

"ATTENTION PASSENGERS: YET AGAIN WE AS A COLLECTIVE HAVE BEEN THIEVED OF ANOTHER ITEM. SECURITY NO LONGER REQUESTS, BUT DEMANDS, THAT HAVE YOU ANY INFORMATION YOU COME IMMEDIATELY TO PASSENGER SERVICES."

I tried to center my breathing. "No," to answer his question and as general commentary.

"NOW, FOR YOUR OBSERVATIONAL DELIGHT, OUR ON-BOARD NATURALIST DAVID GLICK SHALL BE GUIDING US THROUGH A HEAVILY-POPULATED WHALE AREA. HOPEFULLY WE'LL BE IN LUCK AND SPOT SOME OF THESE MASSIVE MAMMALS OF THE SEA."

Grabbing a zip-up hoodie and throwing his arms through it, Jesse pulled the comforter off his bed and opened the sliding glass doors. We scooted the chairs as close as they would go to the plexiglass half wall, and he rested the blanket over both of us.

"Guy'll be happy," Jesse said. "He got his announcement."

"To be honest, I don't give a shit about Guy's happiness."

After a few beats, he said, "To be honest, we'd be warmer in the same chair."

Jesse

Desire, I was coming to find, was like an iceberg, the tip of which was all I'd ever act on and all she'd ever see. We'd be warmer in the same chair was the tip of the whole: you're too far away, I want you on my lap.

"You think there's room for us both in one of these?" she asked.

"We could make it work." The words got a little caught coming up, but the only other option was to reveal too much: *I want you closer to me.*

She straightened at a ripple in the waves, then relaxed when it wasn't a whale. "I'd have to sit on your lap."

I held my hope tight so she couldn't swat it away.

"And then you wouldn't be able to see very well."

"I'd manage."

"What if you miss the whale?"

"Okay."

She stood with a grin I couldn't return. This was serious business for me. I scooted back to make room for her. Facing out, she readjusted the blanket as best she could.

Resting my chin on her shoulder, I wrapped my arms around her. Her hair piled on her head, revealing her bare neck, made this even more amazing, and without trying, my fingers skimmed a gap of fabric at her waist.

The naturalist droned through the PA about whale lives and

biology, but his words were muffled by the space in my mind Navy was taking up. She must have been listening though, because her head was bobbing in this direction and that, every time he spoke.

"Think we'll see one?" she asked.

How could she be focused on whales right now? Her skin was in the palm of my hand. "Maybe."

"If we see one, I'll take it as a sign."

"A sign of what?"

She didn't reply.

"THE WHALE IS COMMONLY ASSOCIATED WITH EMOTION, INNER TRUTH, AND CREATIVITY. IT INTIMATES WISDOM AND EMOTIONAL REBIRTH. DREAMING OF A WHALE MEANS IT'S TIME TO STAND UP AND SPEAK OUT."

"No way," she muttered.

"No way what?" I asked.

"WHALES ARE MASTERS OF COMMUNICATION AND NAVIGATION. THEY ARE KNOWN TO FACILITATE EMOTIONAL CLARITY."

"Okay, that's gotta be bullshit," I said at the same time Navy muttered, "I definitely need to see a whale."

The most kiss-worthy pout slid onto her face.

"Don't worry," I corrected quickly. "We'll find you a whale."

"It would make me feel better," she said.

"WHALES ARE A SYMBOL OF STRENGTH AND PROTECTION, ALTHOUGH THEY HAVE ALSO BEEN

INTERPRETED AS A SIGN OF DARKNESS AND LOSS. THOSE WHOSE SPIRIT ANIMAL IS A WHALE RECOGNIZE THAT WHAT THEY SEE IS NOT NECESSARILY REALITY. THEY ARE ABLE TO NAVIGATE THROUGH THE ILLUSIONS AND INTO TRUTH."

"I dub your spirit animal a whale," I said.

"You don't know how badly I need it to be," she mumbled, shifting on my lap. I swallowed.

"Are you sure you don't want to talk?" I asked. For the final time, I promised myself.

She twisted a little to look at me better. "I am certain I do not want to talk."

Her gaze fell to my mouth and her teeth grazed her lips. There had never been a clearer ask, but she was sad, and unhappy, and searching, and miserable.

There had been so many moments though, and never a good time, which left me to wonder how any time could be better than this.

Navy

"Navy," Jesse whispered.

"Midnight," I corrected.

"Midnight."

"Yes, Jesse?"

"I have been ambushed with feelings for you."

Squeezing, everything was squeezing. All of me was

compacted and tight, on a precipice and ready. "I likewise have been ambushed," I agreed, trying to yank my gaze from his lips.

The naturalist's voice rumbled low as Jesse found my fingers and entwined them with his. I closed my eyes and prayed I wasn't misinterpreting, prayed this was it, begged and pleaded I wasn't making a fool of myself. Then, *sweet finally*, his lips, warm and sure, landed on mine.

Whales jumped in my stomach, throwing themselves into the air—or did only dolphins do that?—and a blazing heat spread from my cheeks to my toes and fingers.

He pulled away the tiniest bit, then came back. And away and back, each time his lips opening more, his tongue dancing out, and God I prayed I wasn't screwing this up. The longer it went on, the less I could contain myself, and soon my hand was gripping his thigh, just for something to steady me, somewhere to keep anchored.

Pulling away to rest his forehead against mine, he smiled. Then came a huge splash from the water behind me.

Isaiah

I paced the hallway as Bern sat propped on the windowsill watching for whales.

How could Navy leave me hanging like this? We had so little time. Would Gram even buy it at this point? After watching them walk out of dinner like they were the only two people on this boat?

I smashed a hand into the nearest photo display, grabbing for it when it nearly dominoed onto the next one.

"Cowboy?" Bern asked, a stern eye on me. "Do you need some soothing?"

"What did you have in mind?" I asked. "No, never mind. I don't want to know."

"Chillax, I speak only of a shoulder massage." He stood to knead knuckles into my back. I couldn't help the moan. "Oh yes, you are tight. What's up?"

I told him about catching Guy and Ethel in bed together, nothing else.

Bern let out a low whistle as I finished. His hands stopped on my shoulders. "That's some high-quality soap opera drama."

"You don't know the half of it," I mumbled. What was I doing? Could I actually do this to her? I guess it's not like I really even knew her. Whatever feelings I had, they were only a short week old. And I had no other choice. I was desperate for the ranch. This was my plan C. The last option.

It didn't feel good. But nothing felt better.

"Do you think Navy's with Jesse right now?" I asked.

"Yes," Bern said, dropping his hands back to his sides. "And I think we're on the wrong side of the boat."

I turned to look at him. "She has amazing hair."

"So do I." He smirked. "Want me to grow it out for you?"

"I could've really liked her."

"You'll never see her again. Get over it."

"I wanted to bury my face in it."

"Don't be creepy."

"Not in a creepy way."

"No, of course not." There with that smirk again. "Let's go get some ice cream, huh? And put our feet in the hot tub while we eat it."

"Because that won't look like a date."

"Who cares what it looks like? We know it's not a date and trust me, hot on the toes and cold on the tongue, it'll be worth it."

"Okay, sure." I had to find some way to pass the time, besides pacing, while I waited for her decision.

Unless she had already made it.

Jesse

I would never forget Alaska, and I would never forget having Navy wrapped in my arms. I'd been hoping for a goodbye peck maybe, maybe I'd be that lucky. And granted I'd have made it a memorable one, seeing as I knew it would be her first, but I'd never dreamed of having her tucked against my chest, us cocooned in a blanket.

It wasn't until her head bobbed against my cheek that I knew it was past her bedtime. Hopefully that meant she hadn't wanted to leave, but I would wake her at a reasonable hour and walk her back to her room like the respectable kind of guy I was.

"Navy?"

"No," she muttered.

"Midnight?"

"What?"

"Come on, I'll walk you back to your room. I don't want your mom to worry."

"Screw my mom," she hissed, her eyelids fluttering open. "You said yourself, she's a bitch."

"I didn't mean it."

"You're right, though. She is." Letting the blanket fall off her, she stood and stretched.

Then she moved so I could stand, and too soon we were inside. It was late enough that my dad was twisted into his sheets, fully clothed. I tossed the comforter back on my bed and flipped off the light as we snuck out.

"How's he doing?" Navy asked, in the hall.

"He says he'll be fine once he's back to work."

"Have you heard from your mom?"

"After thirteen emails. And she only replied with her new phone number and address."

"Ouch," she said, sliding her hand into mine.

"To be honest, I haven't thought about it much the last few days. I'm sure when I get home . . ." I cleared my throat. "My dad's wallowing away his grief hard core and giving himself only a week." I glanced over at her, her bun haphazard on her head and mostly falling out. "And I've been pretending she'll still be there, like this was all a mistake."

She gave my fingers a squeeze.

"If it weren't for you," I whispered, "I don't know what I would've done this week."

As we started down the steps to her level, she sighed. "If it weren't for you, Jess, I might have thrown myself off the ship today."

She was exaggerating, I knew. Still, we'd been each other's lifeboat. There was something to be said for leaning on someone who was also leaning on you.

"Hey." I slowed as we reached her door. "Was this our first official date?"

"Better." She grinned, slow and slinky. "It was my first official kiss."

I caught her lips with mine quickly. "And second." Again. "And third."

When I went for another, she wrapped one arm all the way around my neck, her free hand reaching up to my shoulder and pulling me down against her.

Holding her tight to me, I let go, closing my eyes so all I sensed was the nerves standing at attention where our bodies met. Her mouth on mine. I grinned into her. "I taught you well."

She laughed, and I let my thumb sneak under the hem of her shirt again, just barely on accident on purpose. Only for a moment.

"Kansas City isn't that far from Omaha," I said.

She dropped her grip and a frown pulled at her face, washing away the night we'd had. "I don't really know what's going to happen or where I'll be if . . ." She took a deep breath. "Listen, I need to do something. That whale we saw? He decided it. I'm going to do something and I want you to know it's necessary. I hope you don't lose faith in me."

I tilted her chin up with a finger. "The whale speaks, Midnight. If you say it's necessary, I trust you. Don't look back."

Her frown dropped away for the smallest of smiles. "You really are the best, Jesse. Have I said that yet?" Contrary to her smile, her eyes went shiny and wet, and she squeezed me tight.

It was a lifeline kind of hug, for both of us, and I felt it deeper than even the kiss.

Isaiah

As we headed toward the hot tub, I coughed up my ice cream. Bern didn't bother to help me, not that I could blame him. His mouth was open, and we were staring at the same thing: Ethel and Guy in the pool, splashing each other and dragging each other under like Jesse and Navy had.

Was there more to them than what I originally thought?

Bern fished my phone out of my back pocket, took a picture and handed it back to me. "Send that to Navy. She needs to see this, and she needs to do something about it."

I attached the photo to a text.

"Anything is better than having a step-daddy like that," he muttered.

I looked at him, relieved. "You think?" Because I'd been starting to feel a bit selfish. Like this wasn't a great deal for her, and I should be the decent human, turn Guy in for nothing. Thing was, though, had my dad been selfish instead of trying to please his mother and his wife and his hometown, had he been selfish enough to move to the ranch for good, maybe that would have been better for everyone.

He nodded. "Yeah, I think."

With that reassurance, I pressed send. Even if it twisted the knife in a little deeper, Bern had agreed it was the right thing to do.

Navy

Since leaving Jesse in the hall, I'd stood in front of the mirrored wall in my room with a finger on my lips.

It had happened. *It had happened.*

I hadn't planned on making it happen, like Isaiah suggested, but it did anyway. It did naturally. And then I'd thought, after the first kiss, that it'd be easier to hold up my end of Isaiah's deal, but as I stood there, trying to hold onto the tingle as long as possible, I realized this only made it harder.

How could I kiss Isaiah when I now felt so committed to someone else? How could I do that to Jesse? How could I do that to myself?

My phone dinged and I grabbed for it with my free hand: *Sweet dreams, Blue.*

I grinned, liking that nickname even better than the one Bern had given me. It made me feel better too, not darker than Navy, but lighter and more hopeful.

I responded with every happy face and heart my phone offered. Then added: *I'm going to wake you up bright and early, because we don't have a lot of time left.*

He approved with a long line of thumbs up. Then another ding, but this one was Isaiah.

I clicked into the new text, then dropped my phone like it had bit me. Was it possible to hate Guy more than I already did?

Hands shaking, I marched through to my mother's room. She was sprawled across the bed, snoring, and Guy's side was pulled down like he'd snuck out after she fell asleep. Seeing as she took meds for that, he knew as well as I did that he could get away with anything once she was out.

Kicking the chair on the way back through the living room, I stormed across the floor to rummage in my underwear drawer for Isaiah's necklace.

I would not, could not, stomach this any longer. I would not, could not, stomach that asshole in my life. And after all my mom had kept from me, she owed me that. She would survive.

With the vengeance of a moral warrior in charge of my mother's soul, and the brilliance of a better plan that would work for both Isaiah and me, I removed my old infinity necklace and replaced it with the bright gold disc.

Good riddance, Guy Southard. Good effing riddance.

Day 7: At sea

Victoria, British Columbia

7:00 p.m. – 11:59 p.m.

Navy

I stood in the doorway of my bedroom and watched them on the balcony, my mom jabbering about the fresh gossip from the night before at Bingo. Guy was talking about all the paintings he bid on, but lost, at the art auction with Ethel. My mom asked him how she was, that Ethel, and he replied, "Good, of course."

"Yeah?" She tilted her chin up haughtily.

He chuckled. "You jealous, Pumpkin? You have nothing to be jealous of."

"Would you prefer me older?" she asked, while I swallowed the bile in my throat.

"Of course not. I like the variety."

She grinned. "Variety is the spice of life."

"People, places, things." He held his coffee cup up to toast hers, and she tapped it. "You think Navy will keep her mouth shut?" he asked.

"Of course she will." She glanced back at me. "She's my baby."

I'm sure with the rushing wind and water they couldn't hear much out there, and thus assumed I couldn't hear them from back here. But their voices carried into the quieter stateroom just fine. I spun and left to go find Isaiah. Hell if I was eating breakfast anywhere near them. I may just vomit into my eggs.

Isaiah was in the buffet line, and as I slid up next to him, he glanced at the necklace on my neck. He grinned, dimples puckering.

I put a finger in his face. "No kissing. We're going to have to do this another way."

"What other way is there?" he asked.

Standing on tiptoes, I whispered my plan in his ear.

Jesse

I woke up at three. Three fricking p.m. No texts, no nothing. Had she come to wake me like she'd promised? Had I slept through the knock on the door? I should've given her my key. By the time I ordered room service, jumped in the shower, and ate, it was nearly four, and by the time I searched the ship for her, it was nearly six.

I was the first to the dinner table. My dad, the second. Navy's mom and Guy, then Ethel and Liza. Then, fashionably late, Navy wanders in on Isaiah's arm, a shiny new necklace around her neck.

"Do you mind scooting down?" Isaiah asked. It would stick me next to Delilah and give them two seats together.

Her words echoed in my head: *I'm going to do something, and I want you to know it's necessary*. So she was helping him with his grandma, but why hadn't she just told me? And why had it been such a big decision anyway?

She caught my gaze, her gooey caramel eyes begging something. *I hope you don't lose faith in me*, she'd said.

So fine. I'd trust our night, our moment, and let her help Isaiah have his.

He leaned over and whispered in her ear. She burst out laughing, which got everyone's attention, if they didn't already have it.

Delilah elbowed me. "Looks like somebody's been kissed, huh?"

Navy winked at her mom—how could a mother not read the farce of that?—and said, "Details later."

"Aw, pshaw!" Liza batted her hand in their direction. "Ethel seen you with that pretty boy last night at the pool."

"Because Navy goes to bed early, Gram."

"Humph," Liza muttered.

The whale speaks, I'd said. *Don't look back.* I'd given her my blessing, but even knowing that, I couldn't watch. It was making me sick, making my stomach turn.

Stumbling out of my chair, I took off for the hall without looking back. She didn't stop me. And with my back against the wall by the bathrooms in the alcove, I sunk to the floor and put my head between my knees.

Isaiah

It felt even better than I'd thought it would. Spending dinner curling her hair around my finger, not bothering to talk or eat. Navy throwing smiles at me here and there.

We ate dinner like a couple. Then left like a couple. Only when she saw Jesse in the hall did she leave me. Sliding to her knees in front of him, she whispered something I probably didn't want to hear.

Jesse eyed me. I threw my hands up. He knew my deal, my grandma. No way he hadn't overheard at some point this week, even if she hadn't told him outright. Navy was his, fine. But she was helping me right now. Deal with it.

She finished talking. They stood back up to join me. "Let's split up, boys, and get ready for our last night on the town. I'll text Bern."

As if on a mission, she marched us to the elevator.

"Am I supposed to change?" I asked.

The heavy drag of her gaze sizzled. "Put your drinking boots on, Cowboy."

I frowned. That's how she planned to get through this?

Navy

I'd gotten over my germ phobia and personal space issues with Jesse, but the way Isaiah had been playing with my hair at dinner kind of creeped me out. I just had to get through this night, this one night, maybe four or five or six more hours.

First kiss. First alcohol. First ruse. It was all starting to run together. But the faster this was over, the faster I could get back to Jesse.

He had to understand. He would. He knew enough, and it would make more sense after, when I could tell him why I did it. I couldn't explain more than Isaiah's side of it right now though, couldn't risk him freaking out for Danilo's sake, or his own, and ruining our plans. It had to go down this way, or it might not go down the way we wanted.

Heeled black booties, a tighter pair of jeans for evening purposes, a black sequin tank my mom had made me bring, and my bikini. The sides of it showing helped lend a sexy club type effect, pushing me into a possible nineteen years old, and kept bra straps from showing under the racer-back.

My cardigans wouldn't do, nor obviously my sweatshirts. But my mom's cropped black jacket gave the outfit the perfect juxtaposition, not to mention pushed me to maybe a solid twenty years. I flat ironed waves into my hair, fluffed it up with my fingers, sprayed it with my mom's hair spray, and did some smoky eyes. Final touch was the lipstick I'd found earlier at the ship's general store: Cardinal Sin Red.

Twenty-one years, maybe twenty-two.

I could do this. Or, at least, I *looked* like I could do this, and that would have to be enough.

Taking a deep breath, I gave myself one more pep talk and touched the pad of my finger to the wavy gold disc that hung low on my sternum. No turning back.

It was go time.

Jesse

Dang.

Isaiah whistled as Navy's stateroom door shut behind her, and she strode toward us like she'd dropped every pretense of youth while she'd been in there. She looked like she was taking charge of some ship I hadn't even known needed her. Determined, she swept past us, and when we didn't follow, she twisted around to walk backwards.

"You boys coming?"

Isaiah

I wasn't sure how she got us inside, but she did. A club that sounded remarkably like the bass beat Bern had pounded out of his mouth the night of that mocktail party.

I wasn't sure how she was getting free shots either, but she was. She'd offered them to Jesse and me but we stood there, staring at her. Like we didn't know her. Like she'd walked out of her room a changed woman.

"Is she drunk?" Jesse asked me.

"Probably," I admitted.

"What are you going to do to her?" he demanded.

"Nothing. She's in charge here. This is her plan."

"What *plan*?" he snapped, cornering me, staring me down. As if I couldn't take him.

"Easy," I soothed. "She told me about you two, okay? I'm not taking her or stepping on your toes. She's just helping me get my ranch back. What'd you think was happening?"

He threw a thumb over his shoulder in her direction. "This is not helping you get your ranch back."

"I don't know what this is. Honest. But she made me swear no kissing, okay? You have nothing to worry about."

"It seems I have a ton to worry about."

"Gram goes to bed at ten sharp," I told him. "After that, she's yours. I promise."

He glanced at me, some kind of look, but I was watching

Navy too closely to care. There was so much raw power about her right now. It reminded me of galloping hard with a horse, their muscles burning with strength. Maybe, if I could get Jesse disgusted with her, maybe then I could have both the ranch and the girl.

Breathless, I added, "Meet us in my room at ten and you can have her for good."

"She's not something you can bargain with like that, Isaiah. And she's not something you own."

My eyes shot back to him. "I know. Or I'd keep her. I'm just telling you, for courtesy's sake, when she'll be through helping me."

Navy

After downing my third and final shot, I turned back to the boys and found only Isaiah standing there.

"I explained everything. He understands, he just couldn't watch it."

"Right, of course." I nodded, then stumbled into his very hard chest. "Damn, this was a good idea. This is gonna help."

"You ready?"

"What time did you say Liza would be heading back to the room?"

"Soon."

I nodded. "Okay." But my steps weren't so steady, so I hung

onto him. Right, I should anyway. This was good. If anyone saw us, they'd think the same thing they had at dinner.

One more hour, tops. I could do one more hour.

Isaiah

I slid the keycard in. Navy followed me into the tiny space. My real room, no more pretenses. I was still embarrassed that it was so small, but her smile as she winked at me made it okay.

Besides, we were both so close to getting what we wanted.

Navy

I pulled off my jacket, and Isaiah started unbuttoning his shirt.

This was my idea, I reminded myself.

With both hands, I pulled my tank off and tossed it on the chair, three feet from where my jacket had landed. He slipped out of his shirt and threw it in the other direction.

It was pretty funny if you thought about it. And the shots I'd done put the whole situation in a much more amusing light.

I kicked off my boots and lined them up in the hall. He did the same, putting his right next to mine. We snickered.

He unbuttoned his jeans, and I did the same. His dropped to the floor with ease, but mine were damn tight.

"I might need help with these," I said, a kind of help I certainly wouldn't have asked for a few too many drinks ago.

"Okay," he replied, walking toward me in his boxers, dimple on his side like the ones on his cheek.

"What's that from?" I pointed, letting myself touch it.

"An elk antler," he said.

"Nooooo," I drew out the sound, but not in a drunk way. Or so I told myself.

"I'm a badass cowboy, remember?" He tried to yank my jeans over my hips. I fished under them for my bikini bottoms so he couldn't disrobe me completely, then laid on one of the beds, pushing my hips up to help.

Once they were off, he put his hands up. "I'll be a perfect gentleman, I promise."

I closed my eyes. Right. This was my idea. Go big or go home.

Slinking off the bed and crawling to my jeans, I fished out the Cardinal Sin and reapplied, then turned to Isaiah, who was setting his hat on the desk.

"Stand still," I commanded.

He did. The only things moving were his eyes, following my every move.

I put my lips to his skin gingerly, like he might burn me or like my actions might set Jesse aflame. But we needed the proof, prints of our tryst on his neck, his check, his antler divot. His back for good measure. All for his grandma to see later, after she found us under the covers and thought us naked. After he kicked her out due to our indecency, after I got dressed and escaped.

To see what we had done, when he let her back in with nothing but his boxers on.

Isaiah

"We've been waiting forever," Navy whined.

She was a board next to me, sheet up to her chin.

"The alcohol wearing off?" I asked, because she was growing more and more tense. More and more fidgety.

It was a twin bed. Little space. Nowhere much for her to go.

That was when we heard the key slide into its spot. As the door creaked open, I rolled on top of her, propped myself on my elbows so as not to burden her with any weight. I couldn't do much about our torsos aligning, but out of respect for her—it *was* her idea—I did my best not to press too much of myself against her.

She held tight to the sheet over my shoulders, though my back would keep her strapless bikini top out of view, and twisted her head to look in the other direction. Away from the door. Away from me.

I moaned as the door shut behind her. Well, hopefully behind them. A good one to hammer the point home. Jesse's reaction would only further convince Gram that this was the real deal.

"Isaiah!" That was Gram.

"Navy?" And Jesse. He'd taken the bait.

"*Jesse*?" Navy shrieked.

I peeked over my shoulder. Gram looked, frankly, delighted. And Jesse looked like he'd been kicked by a horse. "Get out!" I growled, playing my part.

"Oh!" Gram put her hands up. "Right, right!" And she pushed against Jesse, forcing him from the scene into the hallway.

Jesse

Once the shock passed, I recoiled from Liza's hands on me, and the only conclusion I could draw was that Isaiah had taken advantage of her. But he'd promised. And she'd said.

Pounding on the door, I demanded they let us in. *Now*.

Liza patted my shoulder to soothe me, but was laughing the whole while.

I pounded harder. I pounded and pounded, then turned to her and searched her pockets for the key. She tried to wrench it away from me when I found it, but give me a break, there were more important things at stake than not fighting with an old woman.

Before I could slide it in though, the lock released with a click.

Navy

There were tears in my eyes, I couldn't help it. Not only had Jesse seen, but my personal space felt tarnished and stripped bare.

"You have to play this out," Isaiah growled, while I finished getting dressed and he strode to open the door on the hall.

Jesse wound back like he was going to punch him, but his fist lost momentum as he saw the lipstick prints I'd left on Isaiah's chest.

Jesse glared at me, mouth twisted, and I choked out a cry. Isaiah pinched me, a reminder my debt wasn't finished yet, not if I ruined it.

"I didn't want you to find out this way," I cried, but Jesse only shook his head. Backing up until he hit the wall, all three of us watched as he took off for the elevators. Nearly ricocheting around the corner, he was gone in no time.

The tears spilled over, and I couldn't stop sniffling. Isaiah nudged me.

"I'm sorry, Liza," I forced out. "I'm so sorry, how embarrassing. You shouldn't have . . . *we* shouldn't have—"

"Oh, honey." She put her arms out, and I fell into them. Patting my back she soothed me with tsks. "It's quite all right. Nothing I haven't seen before."

I sobbed harder. Snot was running onto her shirt and I couldn't stop. I had to believe it would all be worth it, but I felt as low as Guy right now.

I felt like scum. And like I was covered in it too.

Isaiah

"I'll walk her back, Gram," I said, trying to take Navy from her, worried about her shaking body and how cold her hands were. Worried I'd broken her, even though it had been her idea.

"You're in your boxers, Zay," she pointed out.

"I'm fine," Navy said, pulling out of Gram's arms, wiping her face on the sleeves of her jacket. "I'll be okay. Please." She grabbed my hand and said to me, "I'm tired. You wore me out. I'll see you tomorrow?"

I grinned. *Nice touch.*

"And don't forget, you promised me a free stay at that ranch of yours. Labor Day weekend maybe?"

I nodded. *Brilliant.* "Oh," I added, like it was an afterthought. "I'm actually not sure I'll be going back to the ranch."

"No?" Gram asked, hopeful.

"Well, I mean, I thought you weren't going to let me."

She frowned. "A deal's a deal."

"I thought you'd be happier for us." Happier with one less thing to worry about. Knowing I wasn't lying about anything, or denying it. No big inner warfare, no hiding out.

"I'd be happier if I thought you were growing out of that grief you carry around. I'd be happier if you said, 'No Gram, you know what? I'm coming home. You're right. I need to put all that behind me and work toward a better future.'"

I took her hand in mine and bent down to look her in the face. "I promise you, Gram, the ranch is not about my grief anymore. It's home, and I'm not looking back. I have put all that behind me. It's the future I want, more than anything else."

Navy let out a heavy breath, reminding us that she was still there. We turned to her, and she reached up on her toes to kiss my cheek. Squeezing my hand one more time, she said it again. "I'll see you tomorrow."

Then she stalked away. Determined to be proud.

Why she needed determination, I didn't know. She'd done damn well. She should be proud.

Navy

As soon as the elevator doors closed, I sunk to the floor and cried. A newlywed couple and a group of pre-teens tried not to stare, but I could tell they were all sneaking looks. The bride sounded Australian, and she faltered trying to ask me if I was okay.

Nodding at her, I sunk into the intriguing inflection of her accent as she whispered to her husband. Fumbling for my phone, I typed the best I could through my tears: *SOS. Where R U?*

How had Jesse ended up in there? That had not been the

plan. *Oh God, his face.*

Every thought I had renewed my misery, and I didn't know how I could make it up to him. I only had twelve hours before he was lost forever.

Jesse

"What are you doing in the hot tub?" Navy asked, and I looked down at my fully-clothed body.

"I was cold. I couldn't think how else to get warm." I sounded like an imbecile. Like a pathetic loser. No wonder she'd picked Isaiah.

Her eyes were rinsed clean of make-up, but most of it clung to her cheeks and dripped along the tracks of her tears to her chin. She pulled her tank off.

"I had my suit on," she explained, peeling her jeans down with some level of difficulty and stepping in next to me. "It was all a show. You have to believe me."

"The heater in here must not be working," I muttered, unable to get the image out of my head. If it were true, what she said, then it had been an Oscar winning performance on both their parts.

With steady eyes, she moved forward and stood in front of me. "It was all for his grandma, and the only thing I could think to convince her without kissing him, which I couldn't bear to do. I know it was awful, I was awful, and I'm so sorry I didn't tell you, but I couldn't have you talk me out of it or think less of me. I swear I was going to tell you tomorrow, everything would have been back to normal tomorrow. It didn't mean anything, Jesse, I swear."

"Why though? What did you owe him?" That's what I couldn't understand. Suddenly, out of the goodness of her heart? That's why I'd believed it, the so-called 'show,' because helping him was one thing, but what they'd done? That seemed like overkill from a girl who'd written him off so many times already.

"It was the only way he'd place Guy in Ethel's room, if I helped him. He bribed me. Well, he offered and I almost didn't take it, but then I didn't know how else to get my mom and me away from Guy."

Shaking my head, I squinted a little. "What are you talking about?"

"Guy and Ethel are, well, you know, having an affair."

"Really?" Yet I could totally see it. They always sat next to each other at dinner. "How do you know that?"

Crawling up on the spa bench, she rested her belly on the tile and reached for her cell phone. After scrolling through and clicking on a few things, she showed me a picture of them in the pool.

"What does that prove?"

"Isaiah saw them. He walked in on them, in Ethel's room."

I snorted and shook my head. The gall of him. Honestly. "I

thought you vowed to no longer believe anything he says." She put her phone back safely in a dry spot, and I added, "How do you know he didn't make it up to get you to do what he wanted?"

She slumped down next to me and last night came rushing back. This was why she'd been so upset, because she'd thought she was backed in a corner. What a total and complete shit.

"You should've told me," I whispered.

This made her eyes fill, and she turned her head away. "I wanted one night, to not think of it, to have you still believe in me."

"I do believe in you." I said. She sent me the same look she had earlier at dinner, a begging and pleading, as if she didn't dare hope. I nodded. "I do. I absolutely do."

She breathed out a soft gasp of hope, like maybe she no longer believed in herself.

"I wish I hadn't seen it. I wish he hadn't made you do it. I want to punch his lights out." My fist involuntarily clenched again, and oh how I wished I hadn't been frozen in place by those damn lipstick marks. *All the fuck over him.* "I *should* have punched his lights out."

She nodded. "I don't disagree, but we have to keep it up through tomorrow, okay? His grandma gave him the green light after you took off, but she could just as easily take it back."

"Does that matter once your mom sees the proof?"

She didn't reply. It did, because it was her end of the

bargain, and she would uphold anything she said she'd do, no matter the cost. It was her integrity. And I couldn't argue with that.

"He told me to be there," I said. "He made me see it, Navy. Was that part of the plan?"

"Of course not." Shaking her head, her eyes went glossy again. "He did that on his own."

"I thought for second, I thought he'd . . ."

"I'm sorry, it's my fault. He only asked for a kiss, but that felt too intimate."

"A *kiss* felt too intimate?"

"Yeah," she sighed. "I know. I didn't realize what I was getting myself into."

The tub's motor clicked off and the bubbles faded. The silence felt heavy.

"But after last night, Jesse, after you and me, I'm not sure how I could have done it any differently. Wouldn't a kiss have cheapened what happened between us?"

I wiped the lingering tears on her cheek with my thumb. "Nothing could cheapen what happened between us," I promised. "And I'm hot."

Navy

Jesse went to his room to change then met me in mine. With both of us in our PJs, we piled the blankets and sheets from both twin beds onto one, then burrowed under the covers, fully clothed and intertwined.

I was almost asleep, floating right on the cusp, about to fall, when he muttered, "Your fairy dust freckles are enchanting."

My eyelids fluttered, and I forced myself to refocus. A tug of worry in my gut brought on a frown and woke me further. What would he think of me tomorrow, when he found out what else I'd kept from him? And what if I didn't have time to explain?

Reaching one hand toward his face, my fingertip brushed gently against the mole under his chin, and I swallowed hard.

"It's not just about the affair." On second thought, I pulled my hand back and curled my fingers into my palm, as if I didn't deserve to touch him until the air was totally clear between us. "That morning of the train ride?" I mumbled. "Do you remember?"

He nodded. "Something had happened and you wouldn't talk about it."

"I asked you guys not to leave me?"

He caught my fist and loosened it between us, threading his fingers between mine.

"That morning I found everything in our safe. The stolen purse, the chips, the cash, the necklace, all of it. Guy walked in and threatened to take my mom down if I told on him."

His fingers froze, tightened and tense, and he watched me closely, but his expression gave off nothing. I had his full attention, only this time I wasn't sure I wanted it.

"Please understand," I pleaded. "It had been so easy for them to think you did it. I had to make sure my mom and I were safe before turning him in. Then Isaiah told me about the affair, which placed Guy in Ethel's room, so of course I told him, asked him to take care of it and to keep me out of it. It was the only reason he knew and you didn't." Studying our hands instead of him, I added, "I wanted to tell you so many times."

He took in a short breath, like he was going to say something, then released it without speaking. I waited. Finally, "That's what he held against you?"

I nodded, tilting my head down, because this was it. Do or die. After this, what he thought of me might crumble, in the same way what *I* thought of me had crumbled, which already did not feel too great.

"And if I'd told you, you would've done something right away, to fix it for Danilo or to fix it for me. But I had to make sure Guy didn't take me down with him either, because I found the necklace in the safe, Jesse, and my fingerprints were all over it—"

"Shh." He released my fist and pulled my chin up. "It's okay. It's over now, right?"

"Tomorrow morning hopefully, bright and early." I was so tired. So beat. Emotionally whipped, thinned out and empty. But I had to know, even if it was another hit, before I went back to sleep: "Do you hate me?"

"Of course not," he whispered. "And for the record, I would have fixed it for you, before worrying about anyone else."

"But you can't understand, can you? Because you would've done the right thing, right away."

"I do understand," he assured, in a tone so low and sincere that I wanted to melt over it. "Isaiah didn't give you another choice. And you did do the right thing. You're doing the right thing. You're not walking away with a secret and letting someone else take the fall."

"But I was too scared to do the right thing, right away." This was painful to admit, and something that might not have come out at any other time. It was the kind of confession that needed the hushed secrecy of midnight, so when you woke up the next morning you could convince yourself it was maybe never said.

"Everyone is scared, Navy." He pulled my hand to his chest and held it tighter. "It's facing it and making your way to the other side that separates out the survivors."

He said it as if the other side was a given, and like he knew I'd make it through. I could only wish I had that much confidence in myself, and in Isaiah.

Day 8:

Arrive in Seattle at 7:00 a.m.

Disembark by 11:00 a.m.

Isaiah

My alarm was set for five, but I woke three minutes before it went off. I pulled on my jeans, a white tee, my hat, my boots. Grabbing my wallet and cell, I slipped out of the room, stepping over the disembarkment paperwork they'd slipped under our door during the night.

Gram could deal with that.

Navy was window shopping at the dessert counter in the center of the piazza. I nodded to her as I passed. Hoped she'd keep her distance. The point of all this was to keep her clear of suspicion. But I'd told her five so I wasn't surprised to see her.

"Excuse me," I said to the lady at Passenger Services. "I think I have some information on the thefts." No sooner had I said *information* was I ushered into a back office and sat down in a cramped corner. No room for my legs to even fold comfortably.

Twenty-seven minutes later two uniformed security officers came in looking like they'd just rolled out of bed. One of them was Benoît. The other put a tape recorder on the desk.

"You're Jesse's friend," Benoît said.

"You have information?" The older guy—not Bruiser—whispered gruffly. As if this was an undercover operation.

"My aunt was the one whose money was stolen."

Benoît stared while the older guy nodded, prodding me along with a hand motion.

"Well, the man whose wallet was stolen? He sits at our dinner table. They go way back. And the day the money was stolen, it looked like she'd had company, but I didn't know who."

Benoît crossed his arms while his counterpart worried at a mustache the length and curvature of the Golden Gate Bridge.

"I didn't know who else, besides the room attendant, had been in there, so sure, I figured it was the room attendant. But now I know Guy was in there too."

"This Guy, he the one whose wallet was stolen?" Golden Gate asked.

"Yes," Benoît agreed, uncrossing his arms and moving to the door. "I feel you wasting our time."

"No! Wait." Drawing their attention back to me, I hurried

out the rest of it. "I saw him there the day he says his wallet was stolen. If you haven't found it yet, I figured he might have lost it in her room. Maybe even on purpose, if he was trying to deflect attention."

"You were near the first victim in line," Benoît reminded. "Have you been in your aunt's room?"

"You think I'd steal from my own aunt? She brought me on this trip."

They looked at each other, then back to me.

"Listen, I'll stay here while you check it out, okay? You can search my room if you don't find anything in hers."

They waited. But I wasn't going to shoot myself in the foot. I had nothing more. Keep it simple, that's all there was to it.

"Stay here," Golden Gate commanded me. As if it was his idea. "We'll look into it and let you know what we find."

Navy

Benoît and another guy rushed out of the office where they'd led Isaiah what felt like forever ago. One more hour and we'd be docked in Seattle. If they didn't have Guy by then, he was free.

Hopefully he wouldn't think I was behind it. Hopefully he couldn't twist the evidence.

I hurried for the stairs as the officers went for the service elevator. Careful as I reached our deck, my stomach the heaviest pulsing rock it had ever been, I listened before showing myself. When I was sure there was no sign of them, I snuck back in my room. Jesse was still sound asleep on his stomach, one hand trailing to the floor. Slipping into bed next to him, I listened with all my might for the chaos to break out next door.

Ten minutes later and nothing. Fifteen and there was a distant knock. I squeezed my eyes shut and pretended I was asleep.

Then came the shouting. It sounded like a woman, but not my mom. Ethel maybe? A thud against the wall, then my door swung open.

Mom gasped out my name. "Navy?"

I shot up, like she'd woken me. "What? What's going on?"

"Shit, I thought for a second it was you."

"What was me?"

"Why the hell is there a boy in your bed?" she asked, now doubly indignant.

"What's going on?" I asked.

"Security just took Guy. They said they had all this proof and then searched the room, found the scarf he was wearing in the jewelry store, found everything in the safe." Putting a hand to her forehead, she added, "I don't know what to do."

Jesse rolled over and blinked. "What time is it?"

"Morning, you idiot!" My mom snapped. "Get out of her bed!"

"No, don't get out." The booming tenor of my voice surprised even me. No doubt that's what a command sounded like, and its echo lit my resolve like a wildfire. Resting a hand on Jesse's arm, I added, "She has no right to tell me what to do anymore."

"Oh, this is just great, Navy! So now you're going to start sleeping around because your daddy was a lie?"

I threw the covers off of us, revealing Jesse's baggy sweatpants and t-shirt, along with my pajama pants and tank. "No sleeping around, Mom. Just a girl who wanted to spend the night with someone she cared about before having to say good-bye."

"But you were with Isaiah last night!"

"I tried him on for five minutes and that's all it took to know Jesse was the one I wanted."

She threw her hands out. "Fine, I don't have time to deal with this anyway. What do we do?"

"What do you mean, what do we do?" I narrowed my eyes. "We stay out of it."

She started pacing, and Jesse pulled himself to a sitting position. "What's going on?" he muttered. "Stay out of what?"

"Guy's the thief," I told him, as if it were the first he'd heard of it.

He eyed us both and played along. "That's rich. You all crucify my dad, and it was Guy all along?"

Mom bobbed her head like *yeah, well, what'd you expect?*

269

"You wouldn't believe how Ethel was carrying on, Navy. And after all the Bingo I played with her, after all the time Guy spent keeping her company."

I snorted. "That's what you call it?"

Slumping down on the bed next to Jesse, she reached over him for my hands. "Baby, I can't lose you. You forgive me, right? We can do this together. We can get through anything together. Tell me we're together."

A lump charged into my throat but I forced it to stay there, forced it not to develop into tears or emotion for this woman who'd spent every minute of my life lying to me. I couldn't stop my hand from shaking though, and couldn't stop wanting her words to be true. "Of course, Mom."

She let out one sob, then composed herself and stood. "I'm going to try and find out what's happening, okay? You pack my stuff?"

One blink and she was out the door in her bare feet and feather-trimmed black satin vintage gown. Like this was the Titanic and she was on a sinking ship.

I tried not to enjoy that little smite of karma. She was, after all, the one who'd punched the final and largest hole through the story of my life.

Jesse

Navy looked away from the door with a frown.

Isaiah was right. She was a survivor. And in the face of my mom leaving, I had been coasting, ignoring and denying it, whining about poor me and how could they do this. But it wasn't about me. I might be collateral damage, but I was also beside the point. It was time to stand up and worry about what I could actually fix, instead of something that was too far gone and out of my control.

"You did good," I assured, since she seemed so distracted. "No regrets, okay?"

She folded toward me, burying her face against my neck and breathing deep, her exhale vibrating against my skin in a way that sent shivers down my spine. Before I could gather her up, though, her phone beeped.

"Isaiah," she explained, letting go of me to text him back with both hands. "Sounds like it's a reasonably done deal. Everybody wins."

But she wasn't triumphant, or glad, not even very relieved.

"Is there something else bothering you?"

She threw her phone on the bed with a sigh, then leaned over and put her head on my shoulder, loosely wrapping her arms around my waist. "I'm gonna miss you."

I reached for her hand. "I'm gonna miss you, too."

Not that I believed she'd be broken and raw and defeated over missing me, but remembering her face the night before, I could see how she might still be feeling the tremors.

Everybody had won, but she'd paid the full price, and I

couldn't help but wonder what it really cost her.

Isaiah

Aunt Ethel was crying into Gram's shirt outside of Passenger Services. Guy was being strong-armed in past me, and the mainland police were being called to take him once we docked.

"I'm sorry, Aunt Ethel, I didn't mean to upset you."

"It's okay, Zay," she sniveled. "I'm glad you found him out for the bastard he was. I should be thanking you."

"A hero," Gram cooed, patting my chest. "You're a hero. Did you learn that up at that cowboy ranch? It's such a good place for you."

"It is, Gram." I grinned, triumphant. "It really is."

She glanced at Delilah, who was pacing back and forth in front of the desk in a floofy black robe. "Unbelievable really. And she seemed like such a nice lady."

"Well, *she* didn't do it," I pointed out.

Gram visibly shivered with disdain. "It's the company you keep, Zay. You remember that."

"I told you that girl was rotten, the minute I saw her," Ethel nodded, blowing her nose. "The whole lot of them."

I opened my mouth to remind them Delilah had been their best friend this whole week, and to defend Navy, who deserved a whole lot of defending. But it wasn't worth losing what I'd nearly sold my soul to get back.

Navy

It was officially over, and I was officially free, but before I could go I had to find Jesse one last time.

It was a mess on the mainland, all of us dumped onto the same median, the parking lot filing out on one side, and the taxis buzzing by on the other. But I'd made him promise to find me for a final good-bye, and I wasn't leaving until he showed, even if it meant we were the last ones here.

"Hey," Isaiah whispered over my shoulder. Noticing my mom's glare, I tugged at his sleeve and walked us over a few yards.

"Thank you," I said.

"Thank you," he replied. "We make a good team."

"Well, I don't know about that."

A white Jeep honked from the curb, and Jesse hopped out to run over to us. His teeth ground tight as he walked up to Isaiah, but Isaiah reached a hand out and Jesse took it.

Isaiah pulled an envelope out of his pocket and held it out to me. "This is the thousand dollars Guy took from my aunt. She gave it to me for recovering it." He leaned in and whispered, "I didn't tell anyone it was really you, but I think you should have it."

I pushed it back toward him. "I'd rather keep the necklace. This way I'll feel like it's mine, like I came by it the right way."

"You came by it right the first time, Navy," he said. "It was a gift."

"Please call me Blue. And I don't want it like that; I want it as a souvenir." I pressed my fingers to the tiny sapphire on the edge of the disc. "A lot changed for me on this trip." But what more could I say? What more would make any sense to them?

This boat had rocked my life, and the necklace was something to hold onto, something to remember. It was standing up and taking control and facing a past I didn't know I had, that I could barely yet swallow. It was Jesse and Isaiah and Bern. And Jesse.

"I'm sorry, Jess," Isaiah said. "About last night. I didn't think you'd take it so hard. I thought you knew."

Jesse raised an eyebrow at him.

"Really, dude. It was all a show for Gram. Anyway, come visit me next summer?" His gaze bobbed back and forth between us. "I'll put you up in a fancy tent. Has a little heater, multiple beds, space for Bern even. And a legit cement floor with a nice rug."

"Yeah, maybe," Jesse said, very cool and noncommittal.

I smiled at him. "I would like to see the place."

"Come on, Zay!" his grandma cackled from her taxi line, three over. "I told you, you can't trust her!"

I sighed. Little did they know how exposed I felt in that. All I'd been able to think about this morning was how to make my mom legit, how to keep us in one place and not be an accomplice now that I couldn't turn an oblivious eye.

Not to mention how nervous I was that Guy was going to somehow get out of it and that my mom would take him right back.

Isaiah wrapped us both in a hug. Not really my style, but it didn't make me twitchy, which was a nice change.

"Either of you see Bern this morning?" he asked.

I shook my head from inside the two of them. "He texted me 'Good luck and good life.'"

Jesse snickered. "He texted me 'Turn us up or turn us down, but definitely keep us tuuuuurned on!'"

We laughed, and Isaiah let us go.

"What'd he text you?" I asked him. "Ride 'em, Cowboy?"

"Something like that."

"I-ZAY-AH!" his Gram screamed.

"Next summer?" he asked. I nodded and he tipped his hat while turning on his boot heel. Very retro cowboy, I would give him that.

After he was swallowed up in the swarm, Jesse and I made our way back to my mom, where she was inching up in one of the many taxi lines.

"I should probably go, too," he said.

But I couldn't let him, not until I had to. I glanced over to make sure Liza was safely zipping away in their cab, then threw my arms around his neck and held tight, my face to his neck, his curls tickling my cheeks. He lifted me up, onto my tip-toes.

"I told my mom we're moving to Omaha," I whispered.

He jerked away to focus hard on my face. "Really? You think you can get to Omaha?"

When I mentioned it, she'd waggled the fingers on her right hand and said she thought one of my daddies might have relocated there.

It would have blown my mind all over again, if I hadn't been so shell-shocked from the last few days. The possibility of my father being out there and not dead was both thrilling and horrifying.

But more horrifying, because no matter what, he couldn't live up to the pastor I'd held onto for so long.

Swallowing that lump right back down, I said, "She owes me."

"Navy, don't tease."

"She owes me a million times over." I worked on memorizing his face. "Which is a story for another day." Maybe.

I loved how when I said things like that, or when I didn't want to talk, he never looked at me like I was keeping something from him, or lying, or sketchy, but rather like he would wait. Like there was time to wait. Like he'd be around until I was ready.

"Okay, well, call me anytime, text me always, and if you do make it to Omaha . . ." He grinned. "I'll send you my address as soon as I get in the car, just in case."

A beep sounded out behind us, on the pickup side of the

median where Jesse's dad was waiting.

Jesse put up a finger—one more moment—and I waved. His dad looked good. Really good. Clean and sober and spit-shined, as Isaiah would say.

"Wow," I breathed out.

"Yeah. Guess he wasn't lying." Jesse kissed me softly on the lips, but it quickly turned less gentle and more needy. A desperate last, because who knew when we'd see each other again.

"Is that your dad?" my mom asked, sticking her nose between us. Jesse and I looked over at him, his arm hanging out the window, hand tapping against the door.

His face was relaxed instead of pinched, shirt crisp instead of wrinkled, hair gelled back neatly instead of greasy and falling in his eyes, and facial hair trimmed from I-don't-take-care-of-myself to irreverent-cool-is-my-style. He might have even been whistling.

"Yoo hoo, Wally!" My mom picked up two of her four cases of luggage and shuffled through the crowd, across the median, to drop them at his door. She leaned over in her pearls and pale pink cardigan to talk him up through the window. Soon enough, Mr. Kowalski got out and threw her suitcases in the trunk, then came over to get her other two.

"Baby, you're going to have to put yours under your feet, okay?" Mom patted my shoulder. "Or there won't be room."

"What's going on?" Jesse asked, looking from one of us to

the next and back again.

"My mom clearly hasn't lost her touch," I muttered.

"They're going to Omaha too," Jesse's dad said. "We may as well save them the cab fare."

"Cab fare?" Jesse mouthed to me.

She'd sold her car because Guy had a new one waiting for her in Kansas City. We'd been planning to take a cab to the nearest car dealership and start from scratch, another road trip kind of move in the long string of nearly back-to-back road trips of my life. But if we could actually get to Omaha this way, then I didn't have to worry she'd change her mind when some other town we drove through caught her eye by looking 'cute as a button.'

I slid my hand into his and squeezed. "Let's just go with it."

I'd been wrong so many times that week, about what was really happening and even about my life, but this kind of wrong I could live with—the kind that meant seeing Jesse again right now, and hopefully straight through for the next two years. The kind that got me closer to where I wanted to be.

That kind of wrong felt very right.

Thanks so much for reading (you've made it into the acknowledgments ☺.)

If you have a moment, please consider leaving a review on Amazon and Goodreads. It makes all the difference in the life of a book!

For what I'm working on next, check out my website: www.jmercerbooks.com, or to see what I'm reading, find me on Instagram or Facebook: @jmercerbooks.

Acknowledgments

I feel to some extent that I keep repeating myself here, but always and forever I'm grateful to my book people, be they writers, readers, or lovers of stories.

Thank you to the SCBWI community for offering so many tools and learning experiences for writers everywhere. Thank you to my critique group, for caring about craft and making meetings about more than edits. Thank you to Moon Beach for the quiet respite from life you provide us. Much of this book was born there. You are a very special place.

Thank you to Joel, for being you and allowing me to sprinkle some of that into Jesse. I hope our children learn to pour themselves into people the way you so effortlessly do, and I hope the world learns how valuable it is to tell people the positive things you think of them—even to arguable strangers and to the sometimes chagrin of our children. It is a gift, and I'm proud of you every time I witness it.

Thank you to Neva and Aubrey, who are my beating heart, for being you. The characters in this book, more than most of my others, are simply who they are and not going to apologize for it. Be that. Be that and you will unlock the secret to happiness.

Thank you, Navy, for your name; I love it very much. (Or maybe I should thank your parents). And thank you to those who've helped me produce this novel: Rochelle Melander in the editing stage; Karla Manternach, Nancy McConnell, and Michelle Mercier in the proofreading; and Robin Vuchnich with the cover—a great new look to launch a different face with my young adult contemporary work.

Finally, thank you to my early readers! And late readers, too! Without you a novel is sad and lonely. Without you, words and stories are not living, breathing things.

About The Author

J. Mercer grew up in Wisconsin where she walked home from school with her head in a book, filled notebooks with stories in junior high, then went to college for accounting and psychology only to open a dog daycare. She wishes she were an expert linguist, is pretty much a professional with regards to competitive dance hair (bunhawk, anyone?), and enjoys exploring with her husband—though as much as she loves to travel, she's also an accomplished hermit. Perfect days include cancelled plans, rain, and endless hours to do with what she pleases. Find her on social media @jmercerbooks, and online at www.jmercerbooks.com.

www.ingramcontent.com/pod-product-compliance
Lightning Source LLC
Chambersburg PA
CBHW031648100726
47898CB00006B/2017

* 9 7 8 1 7 3 2 1 3 3 2 4 2 *